Silas and the Runaway Coach

Books by Cecil Bødker

(available in English translation)

SILAS AND THE BLACK MARE
SILAS AND BEN-GODIK
SILAS AND THE RUNAWAY COACH
THE LEOPARD

Silas _and the_ Runaway Coach

Cecil Bødker

Translated from the Danish by
Sheila La Farge

A Merloyd Lawrence Book
DELACORTE PRESS/SEYMOUR LAWRENCE

A MERLOYD LAWRENCE BOOK
Published by
Delacorte Press/Seymour Lawrence
1 Dag Hammarskjold Plaza
New York, N.Y. 10017

Originally published in Danish by Branner og Korch,
Copenhagen, Denmark, under the title *Silas Fanger et Firspand*.
Copyright © 1976 by Branner og Korch

Manufactured in the United States of America

First U.S.A. printing

Designed by Laura Bernay

Library of Congress Cataloging in Publication Data

Bødker, Cecil.
Silas and the runaway coach.

"A Merloyd Lawrence book."
Translation of Silas fanger et firspand.
SUMMARY: Follows the further adventures of
a fiercely independent country boy as he briefly
resides with the family of a wealthy urban merchant.
I.   Title.
PZ7.B635717Sk   [Fic]   78-50465
ISBN 0-440-07953-3
ISBN 0-440-07954-3 lib. bdg.

CONTENTS

Silas and the Runaway Coach

ONE

Silas captures a four-in-hand

No ONE COULD say that Silas sat back and let himself be waited on while he spent the winter in Ben-Godik's village. Aaron the otter hunter had straightaway given him his old cottage, which was more or less in the middle of the village street, right where the road curved, and thus probably the one house from which both halves of the street could be surveyed at once. The otter hunter had no need for it himself now that he had married Ben-Godik's mother and moved in with her; he used it only for storing his traps and tools.

To have his own place was exactly what Silas wanted, even if it was just an old, tumbledown cottage, and after he had repaired the roof where it was caved in at one end, he could also keep the black mare inside with

1

him. That suited him perfectly. When he had fixed up the house and both he and the horse were installed, he gradually began to take part in the community, making himself useful in various ways. Not only did he help the otter hunter repair traps and set them, he also gave a hand where it was needed elsewhere in the village, speared eels in the river with the men, and did not walk away from helping those women who had a hard time with barn work. In return he earned his living.

The old misunderstanding between Silas and the farmer Emmanuel, who had once tried to take possession of Silas' horse, was not mentioned. By now everyone knew the story of the wager behind it all and realized that the horse really did belong to Silas, so there was no more talk of the matter. For his part, Silas bore no grudge. Extreme poverty can make people do so many things that they would not do otherwise, he knew that, and there was no point in raking up the past. What was done, was done, and time had smoothed away the episode.

All winter Silas lived this way in one place, trying to act as if he were a perfectly ordinary person, but the quiet life did not suit him in the long run; his craving for change could not be suddenly shoved aside. As long as the weather was cold and blustery, this largely indoor life would do, but when spring first came to the country-side and the thrush began to call in the dank pines along the river and the coots poked deeper into holes in the peat, a great restlessness came over him.

Then for days on end he would roam around on the horse without really knowing where he wanted to go; he just rode, and often it was late when he finally turned home to the otter hunter's old, confining cottage and got his horse stabled. Then he told Ben-Godik how wonderful all the places were that he had seen and what a pleasure it was to sit on a horse again after a whole long winter of not moving about. Ben-Godik nodded in agreement without looking up from what he was doing; however, Ben-Godik's mother sent Silas a long, searching look. She understood perfectly that Silas was surreptitiously enticing his friend, that he wanted to have him along again this summer, but she also realized that Ben-Godik no longer had the same desire. After the old wood-carver had stopped making things, Ben-Godik won recognition among the villagers as his successor and no one tried to force him to look after the village cows anymore. Ben-Godik no longer had anything to run away from. On the contrary, the old wood-carver had handed over his workshop to him with everything that was in it, receiving in return all his meals every day from Joanna. Silas had to acknowledge reluctantly that his friend Ben-Godik was content where he was.

All the same, he really would like to have him along, and while he waited for Ben-Godik to reconsider, he enjoyed daylong rides up and down by the river and far into the countryside. Silas also felt that the black mare enjoyed this wandering life at least as much as he did after the winter's quiet indoor life in the cramped and not-too-comfortable house.

Each day the excursions grew longer, the sun warmer, and the grass more green. During the winter Joanna had helped Silas cut and sew a sheepskin coat to replace his old clothes that were both worn-out and too small.

3

Silas would have preferred one made of otter hide, but the otter hunter had laughed him down, saying that otter was much too costly for the backside of a boy of his caliber: rich and highborn townsfolk wrapped themselves in that. Instead he got Silas a couple of sheepskins and asked Joanna to cut them to fit. As for sewing them together, Silas was sure he could do that himself, and the long winter evenings he had sat hunched over the work by the fire with the others in Ben-Godik's mother's house.

Now, full of joy, Silas sat on the black mare's back and gave her free rein through the landscape, up hills and down dales, through heather and stands of trees, and everywhere birds sang while the still chilly wind pulled at his winter-long hair and whistled in his ears.

Silas competed in song with the finches and titmice. His mouth open and the wind way down in his throat, he raced across the countryside shouting, reveling in the speed, happy just to be alive. Without thinking of where he was headed, without any purpose other than to sit on the horse and fly with the wind, he moved farther and farther from Ben-Godik's village.

Not that he was planning to leave—Silas had not thought seriously of setting off for good, nor had he said good-bye to anyone. But the speed thrilled him so much that on this particular day he reached places he had never seen before, and something further on constantly roused his curiosity.

Later in the day he rode up onto the crest of a hill to look around and from there caught sight of a road winding off into the distance, and since people were not used to many roads in the great open stretches between settlements, he sat quite still and tried to follow it with his eyes to see whether it emerged anywhere else among the hills.

After the intense ride it felt wonderful to sit there with the sun on his back and his gaze far out in the landscape, and before too long Silas fell into a daze.

Until he suddenly straightened up with a start and rubbed his eyes. A coach was careening down the road some distance away, a town coach or perhaps a closed traveling coach—it was hard to say exactly—but in any case a coach of a different and finer sort than he was used to seeing.

But what a way to drive it! The four horses were dashing along as if running for their lives, and the coach no sooner lurched to one side of the road than it swung to the other. Was it being pursued? Perhaps by highwaymen? Or wolves? Silas stared intently without being able to see anything except this one vehicle. There was nothing behind it, neither animals nor riders. Nevertheless, he was sure that something was wrong; no one in his right mind would drive like that, at least not when driving four-in-hand with a closed coach. It was only a matter of time before the coach would crash into something and be smashed to kindling. Were it only to veer far enough for the wheels to enter the soft shoulder at the edge of the road, it would end in disaster.

Silas dug his heels into the mare's flanks and flattened himself forward over her neck, and the black sped down the hill over the short springtime grass, heading for the road a good distance in front of the wildly uncontrollable coach. However, he still did not reach it. The coach-and-four was going at such a clip that it was ahead of him before he got there and he had to catch up with it from behind.

Silas muttered. He had never seen anything like this way of driving four-in-hand. He didn't dare ride up alongside the coach on the road itself; he didn't dare risk the mare being hurt or killed by the lurching vehicle. He had to go back out onto the grass to overtake it and, flat on his stomach over his horse, he managed to pass it.

A man was sitting on the box.

Silas almost missed him, and it was impossible to tell whether he was alive or dead, young or old. Silas had to keep his attention fixed on all five horses; however, he noticed that the man looked very white in the face and clung to the coachman's seat without trying to control the crazed animals in any way. The reins slapped loosely over the backs of the second pair of horses and had already slipped some way down between the lead pair. With their ears back and frantic eyes they stormed ahead furiously while lather settled in white flecks along their flanks, and they did not seem to notice the strange rider until Silas suddenly shot out onto the road beside the lead pair. With a start, they tried to throw themselves to one side.

But that was exactly what Silas had counted on and he swiftly grabbed the headstall of the horse nearest him and pulled it in the opposite direction, thus keeping both horses and coach on the road. But the furious speed did not abate just because he had a firm grip on that one animal, and although he tried to brake both that horse and the others by shouting, it was to no avail. None of the horses obeyed.

6

Silas realized that he had to act, and act swiftly; there was no time to lose. Resolutely pressing the black mare close in alongside, he leaned over the horse he was holding and, taking an extra firm grasp of its mane, swung his leg across its back and shifted over onto it. The strange horse's legs almost buckled from the terror of suddenly finding a rider on its back, while the three others tossed their heads and tugged at their harnesses and the coach behind took some formidable swerves from one side of the road to the other. For a second it looked as if the whole equipage would proceed right out into the grass, but Silas did not let go of the flying mane even though he was well aware of what would become of him if that happened.

Just after he had switched over onto the strange horse, he kicked the mare from him so that she galloped away from the road and the dangerously lurching coach. Silas sensed more than saw her disappear up over a hill covered with scattered juniper bushes, then he focused his attention completely on what he was doing. Still grasping the mane firmly with one hand, he leaned down and fished up all the reins from between the horses with his other hand. Then he pulled in the reins carefully; he had to slacken the speed of all four horses at once so as not to cause an accident. And so instead of shouting and scolding them, he talked gently and reassuringly to the terrified animals. Very slowly the speed began to diminish, the wild dash changed into a peaceful trot, and the coach behind had no more trouble holding the road, although now and then the horses still tossed their heads and rolled the whites of their eyes as if they had suddenly thought of something bad. Silas was able to straighten out the reins and thought that if nothing unforeseen were to happen that might cause panic to flare up once again, the worst should be over.

The boy on the horse turned his head to make sure that the man on the box was still there. It would be terrible if he had been thrown off and had broken his neck during the dangerous maneuvers—even if he were already dead—as Silas could be blamed for it in that case. No one had asked him to get involved in the stranger's plight and his intervention could be seen as taking the law into his own hands, or, at worst, as the onset of a thief's attack.

But the man was there.

Furthermore, he appeared to be alive, for a more ordinary color had begun to return to his face, although otherwise he had not moved. So he had not had a stroke, as Silas had feared at first. On the other hand, it was probably best to let him sit peacefully for a little while longer; he did not look as if he felt like driving right at the moment. Besides, things were going very well as they were.

Silas looked around for the black mare, but she was nowhere to be seen, so he thrust his hand in under his sheepskin coat and found the flute. The man behind him was also wearing fur, not covering all of him of course, but there was fur on the collar of his greatcoat, and Silas would have been very surprised if it were not otter. So he was one of the kind of people the otter hunter had mentioned, a highborn person.

Silas began to play quietly to himself while puzzling over who the man might be, and what right he might have to wear an otter collar. Moreover, could the pelt have come from the otter hunter's traps? There was no way of telling. So he just played his flute, with the reins wrapped around his arm—he didn't dare let go of them completely even though all four horses seemed to be trotting calmly and steadily now.

They turned their ears to follow the flute sounds and Silas waited until he was sure that they had grown used to this novelty, then he blew more forcefully until finally he ended with a shrill signal.

The animal he was sitting on started; he patted its wet neck comfortingly while he listened for sounds from up in the hills. The black was still nowhere to be seen nor did she answer him.

A faint scraping noise behind him made Silas look around.

The man on the box was staring doggedly at him while he groped clumsily under his black greatcoat where Silas caught a glimpse of a long-barreled pistol.

The man thought that he was a robber in the process of summoning his fellow thieves. A thought flashed through Silas' head: What if the man managed to shoot him before he could make him understand that there was no danger?

He turned to the man and smiled.

The man's hands fumbled stiff-fingered as in sleep.

"That was just to call the horse," said Silas.

"What horse?" asked the man, without taking his hands away from the gun.

"Mine," said Silas.

"Where is it?"

"I don't know; she'll probably come soon."

Silas blew the piercing signal again and an even more

desperate expression came into the man's face. Fortunately just then a high, clear whinny sounded as the black came thundering down the hill toward the vehicle.

Silas smiled at the man's confused look. A horse without a rider must have been the last thing that he expected, but Silas played his flute again quietly and reassuringly as if nothing unusual had happened.

But to his surprise he thought he suddenly heard voices, and he scanned his surroundings sharply in all directions. What was it now? Were highwaymen about to attack after all?

It sounded as if it came from behind, but behind him there was only the gentleman on the box and he was not talking to anyone. And yet there were voices. This continued for a while before it dawned on Silas that the voices came from within the closed coach, and that, in fact, people were looking out at him through the little window facing the box. He could see children. It had not occurred to him that people might be inside the coach, for it had looked completely empty when he had ridden up past it. Whoever was inside must have been lying huddled on the floor or under the seats.

Silas guessed that they must be the gentleman's family. It was impossible to see how many there were; the faces were constantly changing because only one or two at the most could see out at a time. Silas was filled with even greater satisfaction at having succeeded in stopping the runaway horses in time, and he no longer thought it was so strange that the man on the box had been white in the face and paralyzed with fright. Who wouldn't have been, with his whole family in mortal danger?

The black mare came up and ran alongside the coach

and Silas could not help comparing her with the four that drew the coach. The sun shone on her coat and her well-kept mane flew from her upright neck. His horse was just as good as the other four, he was quite sure.

Still playing his flute softly, Silas sat on the lead horse, amused by the shifting faces of children inside the narrow little window. I'm driving for the gentry, he thought, but it must be the first time that this highborn family has had a postilion in a plain sheepskin coat playing music for their drive—and one who also has no idea where they are going. He just followed the road, and since no protests came from behind, he assumed it could not be too wrong.

And with delight in the fine spring day and in the successful rescue trilling forth as notes between his fingers, he made his entry somewhat later into a provincial town where he had never been before. Although he had traveled widely in his short life, he had never come here, and he looked around inquisitively.

Even from a distance it was clear to him that they were approaching a big town; the church spires and tall town houses etched themselves distinctly against the sunset, and gradually, as they came nearer, the traffic increased at the same time as the road became broader and smoother. But although Silas had been prepared for a large town, he felt overwhelmed when they entered the streets, and called the mare close to him, and took her reins over his arm for safety's sake. He had never seen so many streets with so many houses all in one place, not to mention the people of every conceivable type milling around. Silas expected them to look askance at him for riding this way right into a town where he did not belong, but he discovered to his surprise that instead of staring at his person disapprovingly, people stepped to one side respectfully, to make way for the four-in-hand and the closed coach. He himself aroused only cursory attention. People bowed and greeted the coach, and when he turned around, he saw that the man on the box was sitting properly upright now with an expression at once formal and authoritative as he nodded to various people in greeting.

Silas asked in a low voice whether he would like to drive himself now and made as if he wanted to hand the reins over to him, but the man merely smiled and dismissed him with a wave of his yellow-gloved hands. He did not appear to be disturbed that a farm-dressed boy was riding his lead horse.

So the procession continued as before, the horses walking nicely down the cobbled streets and Silas playing the flute. He had no particular trouble figuring out where to go; the four-in-hand knew its way now and he could also tell from the people where they expected him to go. They moved right out of the way. A couple of times the horses turned corners, approaching what was apparently the center of town, and then the horses suddenly came to a halt in front of a large house, which Silas took to be a merchant's establishment with a shop facing the street and a portal under the residence above. He thought they must have arrived and planned to dismount. The house was well-suited to both the man on the box and the coach-and-four, so there was nothing more for him to do.

But there he was wrong. The man with the otter

collar asked him to drive through the portal into the courtyard beyond, and Silas saw no reason why he should not do that as well. With a deafening rumble of the wheels, they entered the enclosed courtyard, where they halted. All around, buildings cut off the view from the outside, and what lay behind the portal was at least as large as what faced out onto the street. Silas busied himself with looking around to absorb as much as possible while he was there, but he was interrupted by a boy his own age who came tearing out of what must have been a stable and began to unharness the horses. The stableboy stopped, perplexed by the sight of Silas and the strange horse, but he said nothing. Silas stuck the flute inside his coat and slid down to the ground, then he handed the reins to the young fellow.

"I'm sure you can manage this alone," he said, walking over to the mare.

Great disappointment suddenly clouded the stableboy's face and darkened his eyes. Silas stopped short in surprise.

"Weren't you going to— Weren't you supposed to help?" mumbled the fellow in a low voice.

Silas did not really know what to make of this, but he certainly could help lead the other horses into the stable, so he hung the black mare's reins on a hook on the wall and let her stay there while he began to unharness the other horses. Occasionally he glanced searchingly at the stableboy, but now the coach door opened and out from the vehicle's interior came three children and after them a lady whom Silas immediately judged to be their mother and the man's wife. The children rushed over to Silas, talking and questioning him at once as to who he was and where he came from and many other things, all of which he answered banteringly and evasively. He had to be getting home now and it could not really matter to them what kind of a fellow he was. To him it was enough that he had prevented an accident. Over by the open coach door the man and the lady stood talking quietly together, and the stableboy led the four horses into the stable one at a time as Silas unharnessed them. This took him awhile, for the children went on questioning him and pulling at his clothes when he did not answer; every now and then they swarmed over to their father and mother and asked them a good many questions as well.

The stableboy said nothing more, though it was obvious that something really puzzled him. But as Silas did not consider that he owed him any explanation of his presence, he went over and untied the mare, intending to slip out through the portal unnoticed. Everything here seemed so strange to him; everything was different from what he was used to, the children's clothes and their way of talking, the man who unbuttoned his greatcoat now that the drive was over, so that Silas discovered that not only was the collar made of otter fur, but the entire lining as well, meaning that he had to be a man so highborn that not only could he afford the most expensive fur but what is more he could afford to use it without openly showing it off. Silas glanced at the children's mother when he walked past her, and even though he did not know much about clothes he was perfectly sure that her cloak was also very expensive.

"Hello there!" the man called after him. "Where are you going?"

Silas stopped and turned around, and instantly the three children clung around him again. He must not leave, they cried; he had to come up and have something to eat, he was to stay with them that evening.

Silas looked over at their father and mother inquiringly and they confirmed what the children said, while he weighed the invitation. If he said yes, it would be too late to ride back that night, but then again he could surely sleep in the stable with the horses, and in fact he would not at all mind taking a closer look at a town like this where the churches ended up high in the clouds and the houses were so tall that he truly had to crane his neck to see the rooftops. If he were to stay here overnight, he could see it all in the morning before riding home.

A handyman came forward to help the stableboy push the coach into a building where there were other coaches. The children implored him to stay and their mother came over and rested a light gloved hand on his arm. He could see the bulges of rings under her soft, flexible leather glove and a little lace pocket handkerchief was stuck up into her sleeve.

"Don't leave now," she said, and he raised his eyes from her hand to her face. She was not even as tall as he.

He protested in a daze; he had never before been so close to an elegant city lady that he could smell her. The scent of some kind of strange flowers hung like a cloud around her, making him feel unsure.

But she did not let go, and Silas did not know how he was supposed to go about removing a hand like that, with a glove and rings and everything else, from his

15

arm. None of the women he had ever seen had hands like this. Help finally arrived when the man came over and said that he had given Tobias instructions to put the black mare in the stable along with the others. There was plenty of room.

Tobias, thought Silas. So his name was Tobias, that boy.

Then he said, "I want to put her in there myself."

The merchant nodded appreciatively, and said in that case he should just come right on up afterward, the door was over there and Anna was in the kitchen.

Anna, thought Silas swiftly, glancing at the lady. But no, she could not be Anna, he could not imagine her in a kitchen surrounded by sooty pots and pans— Anyway, it wasn't the smell of cooking she had about her.

Then they all left and Silas led the horse into the stable where Tobias had started rubbing down the others with handfuls of straw.

"Are you supposed to go up to the master's residence?" Tobias asked scornfully. And Silas was suddenly aware that a distance had come between them.

"Yes," he said, "as you heard."

The boy sniffed contemptuously.

"Who is he anyway?" Silas wanted to know.

The boy's contempt rose to undreamed-of heights.

"You don't even know that?"

"No," said Silas, nor did he feel he should have known.

"Alexander Planke." Tobias blared out the words as if the name itself would be a sufficient explanation.

16

"Oh," said Silas, finishing with the mare. The stable-boy obviously felt very superior to such an ignoramus.

Then he asked, "Why are you to go up there?"

"They said I was to eat," answered Silas casually.

"Eat? With the master and mistress? Don't you think he meant in the servants' hall, which is over there?"

Tobias pointed.

"No, he said upstairs," replied Silas.

Tobias shook his head in confusion, there was still something about all this that he did not understand.

Silas smiled in a friendly way, omitting to tell him that it was because he had caught the runaway horses.

TWO

Alexander Planke's house

BEFORE SILAS LEFT the stable he took the mare out of the first stall right next to the door which Tobias had assigned to him, and moved her all the way down to the other end.

"Why are you doing that?" asked Tobias.

"This is a better place," replied Silas. "She can't take too much of a draft."

"That's not for you to decide," Tobias flared up. He was not used to strangers interfering in his work.

"No?" asked Silas peaceably.

"No," said Tobias angrily. "I always put farm horses down by the door."

"She is not a farm horse."

19

"She is too," said Tobias hotly, blatantly inspecting the sheepskin coat and the not especially city-like trousers that Silas was wearing.

"Do you happen to know who owns her?" Silas wanted to know.

Tobias was silent. It did not occur to him that the horse could belong to Silas, nor could he know that when Silas wanted to move her it was as much to get a better place to sleep for himself as it was for the animal. The merchant's stable was excellent but he still did not care to lie right next to the door.

Tobias also thought it was extraordinary that this stranger did not even know who Alexander Planke was, considering that he had arrived with him.

"In whose house do you work?" he asked in order to find out at least a little something.

"No one's," said Silas, which was the truth, as he filled the manger with oats.

"Oh, come on!" exclaimed the boy incredulously. "How else would he have borrowed you?"

"Borrowed? Who borrowed?" Silas patted his good mount on the neck.

"Alexander Planke, of course. The merchant. He certainly didn't find you out on the country road."

Tobias still had an injured tone of voice, but Silas laughed.

"Yes." He smiled. "That is almost exactly what he did do."

"With that horse?" Tobias was compelled to think that the boy was making fun of him.

"Come, come—this farm horse?" asked Silas. "I thought you didn't consider that she was anything special. Anyway no one borrowed me from anywhere. I just caught his horses for him, that's all."

"The four-in-hand? Christ, you're full of lies."

"They were out of control," said Silas.

Tobias did not believe him.

"They were walking very peacefully," he said.

"Yes," conceded Silas, "eventually."

"Then you must be someone's servant after all," Tobias went on, "since you can't just be yourself—no one is. So you might as well tell me who owns the horse."

"She is mine."

Tobias snorted. "Don't think you can put all that over on me!" he burst out angrily. "And that was a lie about the four-in-hand too. No one can stop a four-in-hand once it's out of control."

"Is that so?" said Silas. "Then try asking him; Alexander, you said his name was."

"The merchant?"

"Yes, or one of the others. There were some children too, if you don't dare speak to him personally."

"Japetus?"

"I don't know their names," said Silas. "There was a boy."

"Two," said Tobias proudly. "Two boys and a girl. Her name is Ina."

Silas was not particularly interested in names and said nothing. If Tobias did not want to believe what he said, that was up to him.

"God!" whispered Tobias, running over to the grain chest and hurriedly starting to scoop out oats for the merchant's horses. "He's coming over here."

21

"Who?" asked Silas, craning his neck to see out one of the windows.

"Japetus," whispered Tobias.

Out in the courtyard the elder of the merchant's two sons was walking in the direction of the stable.

"Try asking him," said Silas.

Tobias was silent, preoccupied with his work.

"Aren't you coming up?" Japetus asked as he entered. "Father asked me to tell you to come."

"Yes," said Silas, "I'm almost ready."

"Father would like to speak with you," the merchant's son went on. "He says that if you hadn't stopped the horses we all might easily be dead by now."

Silas glanced surreptitiously at the stableboy, who was pouring oats on the floor next to the manger from sheer nerves. It was obviously not every day that he was visited over here in the stable by the master's family.

Japetus went on talking to Silas in his well-educated city accent, and it did not improve Tobias' mood that Japetus addressed him as an equal, since for his part Tobias had not noticed much more than coarse bragging and peasant ignorance and farm clothing. Could it actually be true that the boy in that uncouth sheepskin coat, which he had obviously sewn himself, deserved such great gratitude as he said he did? There was not the slightest trace of noble birth or city culture about his appearance. Tobias stared for a long time after the merchant's son and the stranger as they walked together out of the stable and into the silent courtyard. Was the farm boy really supposed to go up to the master's and mistress' residence? What if he told on him or complained about the stableboy who would not believe what he said? Tobias' gaze became filled with animosity as he watched the two disappear through the door into the front building.

Annoying, pushy fellow, he decided, kicking a courtyard broom in irritation so that it flew down onto the floor. People like that always want to mix with the gentry. He did not know why it made him so angry to see a boy of his own sort go along with Japetus so easily and casually. Instead, Tobias should have been grateful that the merchant's son had been so preoccupied with his errand that he hadn't noticed that some of the carriage horses still needed to be rubbed down with straw as the stranger's black horse had been. He set about his work sullenly. And when he was finished with the carriage horses, there were all the others, all the heavier cart horses that pulled the merchandise to and from the warehouse. Tobias kicked the broom once more. He did not much like horses. Above all he did not like being a stableboy, but he had to put up with it. His father was drunk all the time and his mother had got him this position because she needed money. He had not been asked whether it was something he wanted to do.

Full of reservations mixed with curiosity, Silas followed Japetus up some stairs and into the kitchen one floor above the courtyard. And just as he had thought, it was not the merchant's wife who was standing surrounded by pots illuminated by the fire from the tremendously large stove, but a big, pale-pink woman with watery blue eyes and white eyebrows. This must be Anna. Her strong, bare arms coming out of her rolled-up sleeves were sprinkled with light freckles and her hair

23

was an even mixture of red and gray. She grunted something incomprehensible when the two boys entered, much too busy with her cooking to inspect the newcomer more closely.

Silas stopped inside the door and took a deep pleasurable breath of the warmth from the stove, but Japetus made him understand that this was not where he should be, and drew him along out into a dark corridor with a carpet on the floor.

Silas reacted with an involuntary feeling of being suffocated. It was like stepping soundlessly down into the throat of a large, shaggy monster. Then he pulled himself together. He knew he did not belong there; he felt much too different from the people who had been in the coach, but since fate had arranged that he could walk right into a great man's house like this, he wanted at least to be able to see how that sort of person made himself comfortable. The otter lining of the greatcoat had already informed him that it was not enough to observe such people—and probably not their houses either—only from the outside.

Fortunately Japetus noticed nothing but pushed the door open and hauled the inwardly reluctant guest along with him into the parlor. And here, too, the young stranger came to a halt instantly right inside the door, this time not because of heat from a stove but instead dumbfounded by the parlor's vast dimensions. Several houses the size of Ben-Godik's mother's could have actually stood next to each other in there. Silas was obliged to collect himself somewhat while he let his eyes run around all the marvelous and fine things; what they were for he could not have said then and there. The

merchant and his wife, or the master and mistress as
Tobias had called them, sat there waiting, the man at a
large table covered with papers and the lady on a bright
little sofa upholstered in a flowery-patterned fabric.

They both watched his entrance attentively and it did
not escape Silas that they sent each other little smiles at
his gawking. He tried hard to get an overall impression
of the experience, but something new was constantly
catching his eye. Never had he seen objects as artistically
elaborate as these.

"Please do come over here," said the merchant in a
friendly way.

Silas did not budge. A big, thick carpet with deep
colors and a complex pattern began right in front of his
feet and he certainly could not just wade right across it.
The very thought seemed impossible.

"I might as well stay here," said Silas right out. "I'm
much too dirty." He cast an eloquent look down at his
not particularly clean soft-soled leather shoes which he
had also worn in the stable.

"That's all right, never mind," said the lady, from the
sofa.

Japetus nudged him in the back encouragingly.
"Come on over here and sit down," he said, dragging
Silas over to a chair just as bright and flowery as the
one his mother was sitting on.

Silas really objected to this but he also did not want
to cause trouble, and since they had told him to sit, it
was up to them.

So he did sit down and had to listen to all the rich
man's words of praise for his resourcefulness and
courage, which had saved them all from certain death.

25

Alexander Planke talked at length about the family's gratitude, for so long that Silas began to feel uncomfortable. His toes curled up inside his far-from-clean shoes, and he did not know whether or not to look at the man. After all, the only thing he had done was to stop the wretched horses, which was nothing to make such a fuss about.

Finally the merchant said that now they would very much like to give him something. Was there anything that he would like?

Silas thought for a long time. There was only one thing that he seriously wanted at that moment, which was for Ben-Godik to want to come along with him for one more summer. And that Alexander Planke could not buy for him, however much he might like to.

Silas shook his head. No, there was nothing. He knew of nothing that the man could give him; he was just fine the way he was.

The merchant looked at him in a friendly way as if full of secrets and Silas could tell from his smile that he had something up his sleeve.

Then he asked, "For example, what would you feel about a horse?"

"A horse?"

Silas was so surprised that he almost thought he had heard incorrectly.

"Yes," continued Alexander Planke, "a boy who rides as well as you and who is brave enough to do what you did for us today really deserves to have a horse."

"But I do have a horse!" Silas exclaimed.

"Yes, yes," said the merchant, "but we thought you

might really like to have one that was your very own, not just one you borrow."

Silas frowned.

"I did not borrow her," he said wearily. "She is mine; I have had her for two years."

Why did it always seem so impossible to everyone that he could own a horse—when she was obviously his?

The merchant's expression became doubtful and almost disapproving. His wife, who until then had not taken part in the conversation, lowered her embroidery and opened her mouth, but then closed it again without saying anything. Both of them studied him wonderingly. How could a boy in a sheepskin coat who looked like a very ordinary farmhand own a horse? Moreover, a horse like that. Farm boys usually didn't own anything. She stole a glance at her husband and saw that he too was at a loss.

So then she asked, "What is your name?"

"Silas."

"What else?"

"Nothing else," said Silas.

"Well, you must have another name. Your father's?" the lady protested gently.

"I never had a father," said Silas.

"Well then, your master?"

"I don't have a master either."

Silas thought of all the times he had been obliged to give an account of his family circumstances, and of people's disbelief when he explained that he did not belong anywhere, either to a name or to a homestead. Why couldn't he simply be himself?

27

The mystery was also noticeably greater for these two, for whom having their father's name in addition to their own was as natural as having arms and legs. In all likelihood they could not possibly imagine going through life without it. They went on asking and asking until they had dragged the whole story of his childhood out of him. About the tightrope dancer who was his mother and Philip the sword-swallower who was not his father but who had insisted that the boy learn to swallow swords like he. And how he had run away and drifted down the river and almost starved to death because he had not had any food for a very long time.

"But didn't your mother ever tell you about some other man?" Elisabeth Planke, the merchant's wife, wanted to know.

Shaking his head, Silas accidentally caught sight of Japetus, who was totally engrossed in the conversation. His expression was completely different now from the way it was when he was pushing and pulling the reluctant Silas into the expensively furnished parlor.

"My mother never told me anything," explained Silas.

"But the horse!" interrupted the merchant. "Where did you get the horse if you set off in a boat?"

Silas explained, but it was difficult to tell whether the two adults believed him. For that matter, the story did not sound particularly plausible. Silas was well aware that it didn't. Nonetheless, the horse was standing down in the stable as proof, though they might think that he had come by her dishonorably, that he had stolen her— for where would a half-grown boy get such a fine horse if he were not employed by anyone?

Without Silas or any of the others having noticed, the two younger children had slipped into the parlor and had heard what he had been telling from over by the door. As soon as he fell silent, they immediately clamored for more stories.

"But Ina and Jorim!" exclaimed their mother in dismay. "Why aren't you with Thea?"

The boy shook his head.

"We want to hear stories too," he insisted.

"Did Thea give you permission?"

The mother looked sternly from one to the other.

"She didn't see us go," explained Ina.

Silas stood up and peered out the window. He said that he had to leave; it was evening and darkness was falling fast.

The whole family protested at once; this visit was far too remarkable for them to have it ended so soon and, persuaded, Silas sank back down on the chair while the two little ones squeezed in on the sofa to sit on either side of their mother. There they sat, their big, insatiable eyes staring at the strange boy in the odd clothes, who talked as if he came from another country. It was much too exciting for them to want to let him go now.

And so Silas went on telling about himself, about how he had come to Ben-Godik's village and lost his horse. A breathless silence fell in the room until Alexander Planke laughed with relief when he heard how Silas succeeded in getting the mare back.

The parlormaid Thea came in and lit the lamps and was horrified to find the two smallest children in the parlor at a time of day when they were apparently not allowed to be there. She immediately tried to take them away with her but both children flatly refused to budge. So their mother let them stay, for they too would surely enjoy hearing what the guest had to relate.

Thea looked over her shoulder at Silas in his rustic sheepskin coat, and blatant contempt pulled down the corners of her mouth. She did not care for people of his sort. How could such a farm lout be anything special? And should he be sitting on display here in the fine parlor simply because he had stopped the horses? Her disapproving face had not changed expression when, shortly after, she opened the door to the dining room and announced that dinner was ready.

Silas stared aghast at the big white tablecloth and all the plates and knives and forks and spoons. Of course he had heard that people did eat this way, but since he knew nothing more specific about how to do it, he hurriedly moved toward the door to the passage with the firm intention of leaving. Japetus stopped him. "You mustn't go now," he pleaded quietly. Over by the table the mistress turned and came back, and Silas saw no other way than to tell her how matters stood. And so when she kindly asked him if he really did not want to eat with them, he said right out that he did not know how to eat that way and would rather be allowed to leave.

"But you must have some food," the mistress insisted.

"No thank you," said Silas. "I am not hungry." Under no circumstances would he sit down at the table and inadvertently do things that would make the others smile.

"But you must," demanded Japetus, taking his arm.

Suddenly feeling that he had walked into a trap,

Silas whirled around and stared hard at Japetus with a look that immediately caused the merchant's son to let go of him and step backwards.

"I think Japetus is only frightened that you will be on your way," said Elisabeth Planke, to make peace. "We would all dearly love to hear more of what you have to tell, but if you don't want to eat with us in here, you are welcome to sit with Anna in the kitchen—if you would prefer that."

Silas sighed with relief.

"But you should know that we do not object to anything about you," continued Elisabeth Planke earnestly.

"Thank you," said Silas hastily, already halfway out the door.

The mistress informed Thea that a place should be set for Silas at the kitchen table, and Japetus ran out into the dark corridor after Silas and made him promise not to leave yet.

Silas smiled and promised. Out in the kitchen he felt more at ease than in among the many marvelous and fine pieces of furniture; out here it was as if he were closer to his own kind, and he looked at the cook with pronounced goodwill. She stood in front of the stove like something unshakable, and although she didn't pay much attention to his presence, she didn't look upon him with contempt either, as did Thea. The strong stout arms swung the pots away from the fire and filled the stove with firewood, while Thea flung an empty plate down in front of Silas. She was both irritated over the extra trouble and scornful because he did not have to eat in the dining room after all. Anna went about her work. The meal came first, before strange boys, and only when a suitable pause occurred in her activity did she ladle soup out for him and put a spoon in his hand.

Silas shook himself luxuriously. Here there was nothing for him to get wrong and although the soup smelled strange and somewhat special, it tasted good enough, and he slurped it down pleasurably while thinking about everything he would have to tell Ben-Godik when he got home.

Anna also filled a soup plate for herself and tasted it appraisingly, all the while keeping her eyes on the row of pots. She never once sat down to eat, but snatched a mouthful now and then while she moved about the kitchen taking out things to be used for the next course in the dining room.

A big platter was filled with slices of meat and beautifully arranged piles of various vegetables. Silas sat there with his mouth watering in spite of the soup. A clear soup like that was not very satisfying, he thought; it was an empty soup full of good taste. Joanna's stockpot was very different, heartily thick with potatoes, carrots and leeks, onions, and chunks of meat from the bones she cooked them with. But here people apparently satisfied their hunger afterward—adding a curious yellow sauce. He didn't dare ask Anna what it was until she had stopped serving the merchant's family. There was no telling what might happen if he disturbed her.

Anna herself said nothing throughout the entire procedure, not even to Thea, who brought out the dirty plates and sauntered off with fresh supplies. Without comment she set a plate with the meat course on the kitchen table before Silas—moreover, it was a clean plate that she had taken down from the cupboard. Silas protested, feeling that he could have eaten more off the one he already had. Anna turned her head and looked straight at him.

"Are you not satisfied with something?" she asked.

"Oh no—it's just all the plates. . . ."

"Now you leave that to me," Anna stated.

Nevertheless, Silas perceived a trace of goodwill in her voice because he was friendly to her. He glanced at the stacks of bowls, platters, and dirty plates piling up, which could all have been avoided if, as in Joanna's house, they put the pot right on the table.

"It must take a long time to wash all that," he said thoughtfully.

"Yes and no," said Anna. "It's all in a day's work."

"I would like to help you," offered Silas.

Anna smiled wryly and thanked him. "No, you definitely must leave that to me. You wouldn't know about such things."

"Oh yes," said Silas.

"Nonsense," said Anna.

Silas got up and insisted on beginning at once.

"Are you daft, boy? They haven't finished their meal yet."

"Are they going to have more?"

Silas considered that an enormous amount of food had already been carried in, and so much of it had come out uneaten that it never occurred to him that they might still be hungry.

Opening the oven, Anna showed him an apple tart that was cooling and a delicious aroma spread throughout the large kitchen. Never had Silas' nostrils been assaulted by such deliciousness.

"I still would like to help you," he said.

Of course he had never had a great deal to do with washing dishes, certainly not with such valuable porcelain as the pile that was gradually accumulating, but he knew more or less what to do.

"I think that would not be wise," said Anna cautioning him, tackling her own food that stood half-eaten at the corner of the table.

Silas believed that he could do a satisfactory job and would not give up. Thea came out with remains of the tart and Anna made coffee and sent that in.

"Do they get so many different things every day?" asked Silas, marveling.

Anna nodded. "They are gentry," she said, giving him a sizable slice of tart.

A second later Japetus appeared and said that Silas was to come to the parlor.

"Right," said Silas, chewing. "I'll just help Anna with the dishes first."

"The dishes?" gaped Japetus. "Why?"

"Because I promised to."

"Yes, but Father said for you to come," Japetus added, not understanding.

"And so I will," promised Silas. "I will just help Anna first."

"No." Anna interrupted the conversation. "You'll do as the master says."

"Why?" asked Silas, turning to her quickly.

Anna stared at him, just as surprised as Japetus.

"Because he told you to, that's why," she said. "He is the one who gives the orders in this house."

"Not to me," said Silas.

Anna started, but Silas made no move to go into the parlor with Japetus.

"You can say I'll come just as soon as I've finished," he said.

"I'm not the one who told him to do this," Anna defended herself. "I'm not the one who's keeping him here."

Japetus felt that the decision was not open to change, so he turned on his heels and withdrew.

"You're daft," said Anna quietly.

"Why?" asked Silas.

Before she could answer, Ina and Jorim crept into the kitchen, where they stopped to stare silently at this stranger who had not come when their father told him to.

Then Japetus returned with a message that Silas did not have to wash the dishes; he could come right on up.

Silas held to his decision.

"But Anna always washes the dishes alone!" Ina exclaimed wonderingly.

"Well," replied Silas, "that is another reason."

All three children stood dumbfounded watching Silas dry glasses and knives and forks and cups, while Anna was clearly at a loss, confused by the situation. Never before had she been the center of attention to this extent.

And then suddenly the mistress of the house herself stood in the doorway behind the children.

"What is this nonsense about washing dishes?" she asked, trying to pass it off as a friendly misunderstanding. "You don't have to pay us back by helping Anna just because you've eaten here."

"That's what I told him!" exclaimed Anna guiltily.

"But that's not the reason," said Silas cheerfully.

"What is it then?"

"Because I think there's so much, because I'd like to give Anna a hand with it."

"But when the master has told you to come—" objected Anna.

"As I said, he cannot order me around," said Silas calmly, "and if I can't stay here in the house unless I obey other people, I might as well leave."

"But my dear boy!" exclaimed Anna, shocked, stealing a glance at the mistress' expression.

Silas handed her the dish towel, and with a little bow to the children and their mother, he stepped back toward the door leading down the stairs. Deep inside he felt that he did not want to give in. Lightly, in the circus manner, he prepared to leave the ring.

"No! You must not leave!" lamented Elisabeth Planke, wringing her hands. "This was not what we meant. We would simply like to learn more about you and your experiences. Won't you come in and tell us more instead of standing here and . . ."

She made a helpless gesture as if what Silas had been doing were extremely unpleasant. She really did not know what to do with this child, who from all appearances belonged to what she would describe as common people, but who behaved as if he were from a refined family. She was not used to so much self-confidence, but he was obviously accustomed to making up his own mind although he looked as if he were even younger than her Japetus—and apparently lacked a respectable education.

"This isn't nearly as dangerous as catching horses," said Silas seriously, thus making her aware that what he had done with the horses had also been on his own initiative.

She understood what he meant and went back to the parlor, silent and confused. She was gone for a long time.

Silas cheerfully went on drying the fine porcelain, assuming that they were discussing his obstinacy and lack of respect. But no matter, he still did not feel servile or in any way obligated to this family. He would not achieve anything in their house, and he had not asked to be received there—he had not even asked to have his horse put in the stable—all that they had forced upon him. Out of gratitude, he thought. Out of gratitude because he had forced their salvation from the wild coach ride on them. He smiled wryly at the thought.

"You should have done what the mistress said," murmured Anna. She was standing with her arms down in the soapy water, not looking at him.

"Why do you think that?" asked Silas.

"Well, because you are here in the house."

"But after all I am not a servant here."

"You might have become one," Anna added quietly.

"Thanks," said Silas. "I can manage on my own. I am not going to be a servant anywhere."

"You lack education," said Anna bluntly.

"Yes, that's quite possible," replied Silas indifferently. It had never occurred to him that that was much of a lack.

Just then Japetus came out to ask whether he would be finished soon, and since there was nothing more to be dried, Silas consented to accompany him back into the parlor.

It turned out to be a long evening. The children asked questions and the parents asked more, and Silas painstakingly told about everything he had experienced over the years both alone and with others. He made the children shudder by telling about the Horse Crone's efforts to kill him in the mill, and he made Alexander Planke himself and especially his wife hold their breath when he told about the boy Jef, whom the Horse Crone had kidnapped and used as a cart horse to pull her knife-grinding cart. The whole family kept their eyes on Silas and a long time passed before there was any talk of going to bed. And when at last the children reluctantly stood up, it was only on the condition that Silas would remain there overnight.

Silas balked at that.

"But Thea has already made a bed for you in one of the rooms," said Japetus.

"Made a bed?" Silas looked absolutely terrified. But the mistress of the house smiled and nodded emphatically.

"I could sleep in the stable just as well," protested Silas.

He had nothing against spending the night in the merchant's place, but he wanted to go out and look around the town in the morning. In the long run he was bored just sitting and talking about everything that had happened; he would much rather go out and experience something new, and a town like this would certainly have something to offer.

"There'll be no discussion," said Elisabeth Planke

decisively. "We don't let a guest sleep in the stable, and as Japetus said, a bed has been made up for you."

Silas considered this a moment; he felt almost as if he were about to be put in some kind of confinement, and he would have much preferred to sleep near the horse so that he could have simply got up and disappeared early in the morning. But then he thought of what Anna had said, that he lacked education and manners, and he had to grant her that it certainly wouldn't be well-mannered or educated just to leave when people had been decent to him in other respects. Mightn't it be more polite to have the matter out? He decided to give it a try and said right out that he had never been in a city like this one before and that he would like to go out and look around in the morning before he left instead of just sitting and talking.

"Well," said Alexander Planke, "that sounds reasonable. I would certainly want to do that too if I were you, but still there is no need to sleep in the stable. A room has been prepared for you in the attic and in the morning Japetus can go with you; he knows the town and he can show you what is worth seeing."

This sounded all right to Silas; and that was that.

THREE

Carnelian

THE NEXT MORNING Silas woke early. He was not used
to lying in bed for long, and the strange surroundings
also helped shorten his sleep. It had only just begun to
grow light when he stood up on the only chair in the
room and stuck his head out the window in the roof. The
chill dawn air streamed in, and his skin, warm from the
night, turned to gooseflesh, but he stood there for a long
time trying to get his bearings. The long stairs that
wound all the way up through the house had turned
him around so many times that he no longer had any
idea of the points of the compass. Nor did he know
whether the stairs were the only way down and he had
no idea who was sleeping behind all the closed doors
in the attic corridor. None of this worried Silas, but he

usually made himself familiar with his surroundings as soon as he came to a new place. He thought it was always good to know a little in case something came up and he suddenly had to get away quickly.

From up there he could see many rooftops and after some scrutiny he became convinced that the nearest roof must be that of the back building facing the courtyard, where his horse was stabled on the ground floor. The courtyard itself could not be seen, but since there were several windows with wooden shutters and since the end of a joist with a block and tackle jutted out from the masonry above the topmost one, he concluded that the other floors were the warehouse, where goods were hauled up by rope and pulled in through the windows.

The other roofs he could not identify, and he drew his head back in and closed the little iron window. The room he had been given had slanting walls; it was not large and was probably intended for a servant girl, at least judging from the spartan furnishings. The iron bed under the eaves had been painted white at one time, but not much paint was left on the thin iron trim of the frame, and the chair he had just stood on had also known better days. In one corner there was an iron stand with a water pitcher and basin, and when he discovered water in the pitcher and a striped hand towel on a nail in the wall he splashed water on his face and then dried it. After all, they shouldn't get the idea that he did not know what such things were for. He also had something to tidy his hair with. Joanna had broken her big, yellowish bone comb at one point during the course of the winter; Silas and Ben-Godik had each appropriated half. Silas kept his piece in the leg of his gray striped sock. He took it out now and inspected himself in the little mottled mirror over the washstand. His hair was long—definitely longer than usual since he had not cut it all winter—and tended to curl up at the ends, otherwise it would have reached his shoulders. It was as matted as a horse's mane that has not been currycombed all summer and he almost immediately gave up tugging the comb through it and stuck the comb back in his sock. But then he thought of how Japetus' hair looked and of how, if this hair had actually belonged to a horse, he would not have given up on it so fast. And it occurred to him that maybe he could do something about all those mats and tangles.

He decided to go downstairs.

There was still not a sound to be heard anywhere in the house, and it was bound to be a long time before he had any breakfast and before Japetus appeared. Apparently people did not get up as early here as they did out in the country, but then of course they also didn't have any cows to milk either. Even though it was quiet, he wanted to go downstairs anyway. Surely he would be allowed to go over to the stable.

Silas took one last look around the little room to see whether he had forgotten anything, but as there was nothing he quietly opened the door a crack and slipped out into the long passage, which he had only glimpsed fleetingly when he had been shown up by the glow of a tallow candle the night before. Now he could see the whole row of doors leading to a whole lot of rooms on either side, many more rooms than there were servants, he thought—but perhaps these were also for travelers to spend the night in. People who would come to town from the surrounding countryside to do business. He did not know that for sure, but in any case the merchant's family did not sleep up here, that much was certain.

The stairs creaked and Silas tried to step as quietly as possible. In fact, it suited him perfectly that no one was up and about yet because he could have a little look around on his own.

Down by the entrance to Alexander Planke's apartment he stood awhile listening at the kitchen door. He could fancy a slice of bread, but since no one was clanking pots at the stove or anything else, he continued on down to the door leading out into the courtyard. It was bolted and had a massive iron bar across it as well. Silas considered whether it would be all right to open it, since he would not be able to lock it behind him. Someone could get into the house while he was outside.

While he was deliberating, his glance fell on another door leading in the opposite direction. It was incredibly much the worse for wear, and Silas surmised that it led into the shop. Japetus had told him about the shop where they sold every conceivable thing, but Silas had not seen it yet. He tried the door carefully, and as it readily opened, he decided to go right on in and look around a little while, waiting for the right time to go over to the stable. Very softly he closed the door behind him and slipped into a wonderful dimness that smelled special and spicy, where marvelous objects faded away in the corners or hung under the beams of the ceiling.

The wheel of a coffee grinder was silhouetted by the window. Silas stopped in the middle of the floor and looked around and sniffed. It was so difficult to see anything that he had to sniff his way around to find what was there. Tar, he thought, and ropes and salted herring and cheese. He could smell more things than he could see, and he sniffed around the room as quietly as he could without stumbling too much.

Slowly he moved around behind the counter and looked at all the drawers that had small white labels on them with letters showing what they contained. Silas could not read; instead he smelled a couple of drawers and stuck his nose in them.

And while he was standing like that suddenly a hand closed tight around his ankle like an iron band.

Silas could not do anything before his legs were pulled out from under him and he lay on the dusty wood floor with a male figure above him.

"Well, well," said a voice, "you certainly weren't expecting that."

Silas did not reply; both his arms were twisted behind his back and his face pressed down against the hard floor. It had all happened so fast that he had not even seen the person who overpowered him.

"So you go around sniffing into other people's things at night, do you?" continued the voice.

"Let me go," protested Silas. "I'm a guest in this house."

"Is that so?" said the voice. "And isn't this a fine way to be a guest!"

"Do you think I'm a thief?" hissed Silas angrily.

45

"I can't see what else you'd be doing in the shop in the middle of the night."

"This isn't the middle of the night. I just wanted to look around, and it isn't my fault that people take so long to get up here in the city."

"Would you have me believe that?" said the voice.

"Ask the merchant himself. I saved his life yesterday, and he himself told me to stay."

Silas was annoyed that it took so long to convince this fellow.

"You'll enjoy telling all this to the merchant," said the voice sarcastically.

"But it happens to be true. I was the one who stopped the horses yesterday."

"Then you certainly didn't have to break in."

"I didn't break in," replied Silas. "The door was open."

"So much the worse," the voice judged. Silas twisted his head around to see who it was.

"Now you'll have to wait here until someone comes, and God help you if you should try to get away, for I'll be obliged to hit you and I only hit once."

"Then couldn't you hold me by my legs instead? I'm going to earn my living playing the flute, which will be rather difficult if you break my arms off at the shoulders."

"Like hell I will," swore the voice. "You just mean to escape."

"I do not," Silas continued. "I haven't taken anything. And I'm not sure the mistress will be very grateful to you for having ruined my arms."

"You should have thought of that awhile ago. It's my

46

job to catch thieves in Alexander Planke's shop at night."

"But I've never seen a shop before," wailed Silas, "and since I was sleeping up in the attic anyway and was awake, and since I couldn't go out because the door was locked . . . if you'll hold me by the legs instead, I'll play my flute for you while we wait for someone to wake up."

Easing his grip on Silas' arms, the man grabbed his ankles instead and Silas struggled up to a sitting position.

"You're much too strong," mumbled Silas, rubbing his wrists and wiggling his fingers while he leaned back against the labeled drawers of merchandise. "This is almost like getting your arms caught in a fox trap."

The fellow grinned and Silas saw that it was the handyman who had helped with the coach the day before.

"No one has ever got away from me so far," said the handyman with satisfaction.

"Do people often break in?" asked Silas.

"Oh yes, it does happen."

Silas was impressed that the handyman was so strong because he was by no means young nor was he especially big or muscular.

"It's all in the hold," explained the man. "I learned it from a friend who got it from a Chinaman."

Silas rubbed his arms thoughtfully.

"A man can kill someone with his bare fists," continued the fellow, since Silas had not commented, "if he knows how."

Silas shuddered.

"Have you ever tried?" he asked.

47

"No—not seriously."

"Or even for fun?" asked Silas.

"You've forgotten to play," said the handyman as if to change the subject.

"I would just like to know for whom I am playing first," stated Silas.

"Me, of course."

"I don't know who you are."

"You saw me yesterday."

"That tells me nothing about your name."

"Carnelian," said the man.

"What?" said Silas.

"Carnelian," repeated the other.

"Is that a name?" asked Silas incredulously.

"Some people think so."

"It sounds like a city with water in the streets," said Silas thoughtfully.

"You mean like a flood?"

"No, as if it's meant to be there . . . wet stones and bridges. I like it."

"But unfortunately you left your flute somewhere, right?"

"Why do you think that?" asked Silas, looking straight at the man in the light that was gradually beginning to filter in through the windows.

"And you have to go get it, right?"

Silas smiled and fished the flute out from under his coat.

"No," he said, "but I am about to starve."

"You have to wait awhile longer," judged the man.

Silas began to play. They went on sitting on the floor

48

behind the counter and in the early dawn light Silas could understand better why he had not heard a sound from the man before he was aware of being grabbed by the ankles. The man had been sleeping under the long counter; his blanket lay halfway out onto the floor; all he had to do was reach out an arm to catch hold of the supposed thief.

"Play music about that city with water in the streets," requested the handyman, listening to the flute which instantly changed to wet, rippling sounds. Sure enough, he had seen the boy the previous day and had heard that he had stopped the four-in-hand, but around town they said that he had used a flute to control the bolting horses, and Carnelian had not wanted to believe that— until now.

Silas played softly and dreamily. He had never seen a city with water in the streets, but he sat quite still and built one up for his inner eye; everything that he knew about water and houses and sailing ships and sun he summoned up, and the strong handyman felt his heart melt within him. An almost forgotten childhood in a distant land came back to him, and he too pictured small wavelets licking up against sunbaked walls. There had been a city once where you sailed right up to the doors in the same way that others ride up and bring their horses to a halt.

Silas had heard of such a city and the handyman's singular name had pulled the tale out of his mind; he did not know whether it was true, or only the legend of some place that had existed once in the past, or a dream. But he created it there in Merchant Planke's

49

shop among the smells of chewing tobacco and dried
fruits and he played for a long time while he imagined
the land where it could be found.

Suddenly he discovered that Carnelian's head had
sunk down onto his chest. Still playing, he moved his
foot away from the man's hand and stood up. The man
slept soundly and Silas vanished silently by the same
door through which he had entered.

Out on the stairs he removed the bar from the door
and stepped outside. It was not dangerous to leave it
open now; the sun was already shining on the surrounding roofs and some chimneys were beginning to smoke.
Silas walked over to the stable and made sure that the
mare was well. He actually wanted to talk with Tobias,
but the boy was snoring loudly inside the tack room and
Silas left him alone and patted the mare's neck instead.

Just as his fingers touched the mane he got to thinking
of his own hair and went over to the windowsill where
the currycombs lay. His hair should look neat if he were
going out around town with Japetus, he thought, brush-
ing it hard. After that he found it easy to comb and then
he felt with his hands to make sure it was smooth and
tidy. He had no mirror.

Then he contemplated going up into the warehouse
but the incident over in the shop made him decide not
to. After all, he was not sure he would get away so
lightly next time, and to appear like an intruder and
thief to the merchant was not what he cared to do.

Out in the courtyard Anna appeared, carrying the ash-
pan from the stove which she emptied onto the rubbish
and manure pile. He hurried out and saw her brighten
at the sight of him, and he followed her confidently up

50

into the big kitchen where a good fire was already crackling in the stove. Anna warmed a spot of coffee from the day before and cut a couple of slices of a mixed rye-and-wheat loaf. She said that she was not too busy at the moment and allowed herself time to sit awhile on a stool and slurp the hot coffee, cupping her hands around it.

Silas waited until she had drunk it all and eaten one of the pieces of bread. It was only a question of not beginning too soon, he knew that, as he chewed energetically and gulped his coffee.

Then he asked, "Who is Carnelian?"

Anna looked at him over the rim of her cup as if she did not really know what to answer.

Then she said, "He sweeps the courtyard and the street and things like that." But she suspected, rightly, that this was not exactly what Silas wanted to know.

"I mean who is he, where does he come from and things like that?" Silas asked again.

Anna stared distantly in front of her. Then she said, "That no one knows. He came to town when he was quite little, that was before I was born, and people say that he talked a foreign language which no one understood. He did not look like other children here either, not his clothes or anything."

"How did he come?" Silas wanted to know.

"I don't know—and he doesn't really know that himself either, but someone must have brought him. No one here in town saw him with his own people; he was just suddenly here—sitting in the gutter and living wild like a dog."

"You can see that in him," said Silas.

51

"Maybe—but you can't hear it anymore. He never talks about it himself."

"And now he stays here in town?" asked Silas.

"Not all the time; he has been away several times. They say that he sailed away somewhere, but he doesn't talk about that either. Mostly, he says very little."

"He caught me this morning," said Silas.

Anna's eyes took on a watchful expression over the rim of her cup.

"Caught you how?"

"Down in the shop. I went in to see what it was like."

"But then how did you get away? He never lets anyone he has caught get away."

Silas told her and Anna poured more coffee.

Then she said, "He may not talk about that either. He cannot bear to have anyone outwit him, but he greatly admires those who can."

"Most people want revenge," said Silas thoughtfully.

"Not Carnelian," Anna stated, and that settled that.

"You seem to know him well."

Anna smiled enigmatically.

"That depends on how you take it," she said.

Silas sat awhile slurping coffee noisily and munching bread.

"Maybe you came from the same place?" he asked later, knowing at the same time that she had not. She was just as fair and blue-eyed and ruddy as the other was dark and brown-eyed.

"Mmm," said Anna.

Silas waited silently.

"No, you see, I was almost born into this, into this

house I mean. I don't come from anywhere; my mother was cook here before me and I came into the world in this very street. I was never meant to wander far from here."

Silas felt he could detect a faint sigh behind her words.

"Have you never traveled?" he asked wonderingly.

"Places," she said emphatically, "are something you hear about. The master and mistress must have their meals on time."

"But have you never been away from this town?" Silas went on.

"No further than where I could always be sure to get back to prepare the next meal."

Silas sat there trying to imagine what it would be like to live in the same house all the time, not just for one winter but for every winter and every summer the whole of one's life. He did not understand how anyone could endure that, for it must feel like imprisonment. Never to be able to say good-bye and set out to see something new. Never to change place, change people, change life. Silas could not imagine what it must be like; he had never tried it, but those who could endure it must be made a different way than he was. Not even in a large and wealthy house like this could he contemplate spending the rest of his days.

But Anna could, even though he had noticed in her voice some slight longing for a way out. She stayed— and perhaps basked a little in the glow of foreignness surrounding Carnelian.

And Elisabeth and Alexander Planke could. They

would certainly never feel an urge to go on and on in some direction when they went out for a drive. They would want to turn back.

And Japetus?

Japetus was always so polite and well-behaved that it was impossible to know what he was really like—what he thought and felt inside, or what he might want to do.

Then he asked, "Has Japetus never been anywhere else either?"

"You mean to live?" she asked. "Well, all the children have visited relatives now and then."

"But has he never traveled anywhere alone?" Silas wanted to know.

"Lord preserve us! No, why should he do that? He is much too young to look after himself."

"He is older than I am," observed Silas.

Anna turned her head.

"But, you see, there is something different about you."

Silas got up and thanked her for the meal and thought that she was probably right. Then he went down to the stable to see whether Tobias was awake.

Down in the yard he met Carnelian, who winked his golden eye in something partly resembling an acknowledgment and partly like a crafty smile. Silas grinned and the man shook his head in resignation.

"It must be my age," he murmured as Silas passed him.

"Anna sends greetings," Silas murmured in return. "If you hurry she has coffee and rye bread."

Carnelian acted as if he heard nothing, but from inside the stable Silas could see him steal over to the back stairs and vanish inside.

Tobias was currying the merchant's horses, but even though he was standing on his feet and moving his arms, it still looked as if he were fast asleep.

"What are you staring at?" he snapped when he noticed that Silas was observing his slow working tempo.

"It doesn't look as if you get too much pleasure from what you're doing," said Silas kindly.

Tobias cursed every horse on the face of the earth.

"I loathe the critters," he admitted.

"Why?" Silas wanted to know.

"Because I want to work in the shop," said Tobias contrarily. "This is no good; it's the same day after day."

"You'd rather stand over there selling syrup and salted herring and pouring cinnamon into little twists of paper?" Silas was on the brink of smiling but checked himself; there was no doubt that the boy was serious.

"Well, at least it isn't as filthy as here," grumbled Tobias, kicking a pile of horse droppings so that they flew in all directions.

"The only filth is your own doing," Silas stated, taking the currycomb from the boy's hand and continuing where he had left off.

"Anyway, I like horses," he said.

"Then you can have this glorious position if you can get the merchant to place me over in the shop," said Tobias. "You can send him my greetings and say that I'm remarkably better at doing sums and counting money than I am at hauling horse manure."

"Why don't you tell him yourself?"

"Are you crazy? Do you think I want to be fired?"

"Then why not tell Japetus?" Silas asked, starting on a new horse.

"Aw, Japetus," Tobias wrenched the name out of his mouth with a grimace. "He is hardly someone you can talk with."

"Have you tried?"

"As if he thought a stableboy counted at all," Tobias flared up. "Do you think he ever looks in my direction —or ever says anything?"

"You should explain to him that a bad stableboy brings no profit to a fine merchant's establishment."

"Oh yes, great," fumed Tobias. "Then they'd throw me out. I have to earn money; my mother is ill. Tell them I'm a bad stableboy! Ha! You don't know very much about city life, I can tell."

"But don't you think they need an apprentice in the shop?"

"Who would I hear that from?" Tobias flared up again. "No one tells me anything about what they need. Even if they did, there are plenty to choose from."

Silas curried for a while in silence.

Then he said, "Horses really should be looked after by someone who likes them. That's what's best for them."

"Just don't try to get me thrown out because of that," Tobias threatened him. And Silas could hear that he already regretted what he had said.

"Didn't you just say that you'd rather be over in the front building selling kerosene?" Silas looked at him questioningly.

"I might as well wish for a piece of the moon," said Tobias, hurt and annoyed. "I might as well—I might as well—"

"Wish," Silas added, since Tobias was unable to come

up with anything. "As long as you keep wishing, you stand a chance. . . . But there's also no harm in taking extra good care of the horses while you wait for your wish to come true. You might as well make it clear to everyone that you are an especially good and careful worker."

Tobias just glared at him.

Was Silas making a fool of him? What should he believe? He sounded so convincing, so definite—such a strange, farm-dressed young fellow who wasn't even as old as himself? Thoughts churned inside Tobias' head. There was no knowing who this strange boy really was. After all, he had actually slept upstairs in the front building and he was invited into the parlor—and he had a horse of his own. What if he also were not lying?

Later, when Silas walked past, he could hear Tobias whistling while he eagerly lit into the horse droppings with the shovel as if a golden apple had been buried among them.

FOUR

An offer

SILAS RETURNED TO the kitchen and asked Anna what time Japetus usually got up.

"I believe the master and mistress would like you to join them for breakfast," said Anna instead of answering his question. At the same time she turned away from the stove and stared fixedly at him with an expression that clearly showed her determination to block any protest.

"They want to talk with you," she said.

Silas was about to ask her to go to the parlor and say that he had already gone out into the town when he caught sight of her face. He couldn't help smiling.

"You look like a dog that would fly at my legs if I go anywhere near the door," he said.

Anna's expression did not change.

"You don't have to look like that," he went on. "What am I supposed to do?"

"Eat breakfast with them. They want to talk with you."

Silas looked at her out of the corner of his eye.

"Has Carnelian told on me?" he asked.

"He never tells on people; you should know that," Anna burst out in an injured tone.

"Then what is it?"

"Shouldn't they tell you themselves?" Anna asked in return.

"But I don't want to sit all day on display like an ornament," objected Silas. "I want to go out and see the town."

"And so you will," Anna assured him.

Silas sighed and Anna took a deep breath of relief. She had strict instructions not to let him get away.

"Now you had better just wash your hands," she said.

Silas looked at his hands.

"What's wrong with them?"

"Haven't you been in the stable?"

Silas admitted that he had.

"There's soap over by the sink," said Anna.

Silas trotted over obediently and washed his fingers and dried them under his arms.

"You'll find a towel hanging there," Anna informed him.

Silas took it.

"You might also comb your hair," she went on mercilessly.

"I've done that."

Silas shook a couple of wisps of hair away from his forehead.

"It must have been a long time ago."

"Well, when I got up."

"You'd better do it again. The mistress appreciates people who look tidy at the table."

Silas felt like informing the cook that he was fairly indifferent to what the mistress appreciated, when his glance fell on everything that Anna had amassed on the tray and the table beside it. There were both bread and rolls, jam and honey, eggs and sausages, and it was as if the very sight cut short his protests.

"Gosh, do they eat all this in the morning?" he said.

Anna concealed a smile and went in with a tray, while Silas fished out his comb again and thrashed it through his curls.

"Not in the food!" shrieked Anna when she came out again and saw him.

Startled, Silas looked around; he wasn't touching anything.

"Your hair," she said. "People don't comb their hair near food."

"You certainly take everything very seriously," Silas commented, sticking the comb back in his sock while Anna looked him over.

"You'd better go in now," she said.

Silas went into the dining room. No one was there, and he walked over to the window and looked down at the street. Anna came and went, carrying the last things.

Suddenly Japetus burst into the room from the opposite end headed for the kitchen. He seemed in a hurry; as he rushed by he turned his head toward the shadow by the window and then he stopped abruptly.

"There you are!" he exclaimed with every indication of surprise.

"Yes," said Silas.

"It's just that Father said I was to find you. I didn't know you were here."

"Anna told me," explained Silas. "She said your father wanted to talk to me." He studied the boy's expression to fathom his mood, but Japetus seemed cheerful and lively, brimming full of anticipation.

Over in the background Elisabeth Planke helped a little old lady through the door.

Silas had not seen her before, and Japetus explained that she was Granny.

"Granny?" inquired Silas.

"Yes, my father's mother, Nicoline Planke. Actually, the house and shop belong to her."

And so does her family, thought Silas, with an extra glance at that old lady's sharp nose and keen eyes. In a flash he understood why Japetus could not do anything on his own, why he couldn't simply go down to the stable, take a horse, and ride off. He was not his own man; he belonged to the family; he was attached to it the way the last joint of a finger is attached to a hand. It was a kind of imprisonment.

The old lady was brought over and seated at the table and Elisabeth Planke said good morning to Silas and asked him to sit down as well. "The others are coming shortly," she said. Granny's cane was propped in the corner by the door, and Silas chose a chair a safe distance from that sharp nose.

Cautiously he shoved his legs in under the white tablecloth and sat down. On top of each trencher lay a small rolled-up piece of cloth which Anna had called a napkin, telling him that it was used to dry one's mouth. Incredible how they could make everything so complicated in this house. Why should it be finer to do things the hard way, when of course it would be far easier to wipe your mouth on the back of your hand and then rub your hand on your trouser leg. He had always done that and everyone he had ever eaten with had always done that until now. This other way was nonsense, in his opinion.

Still there was something alarming about such a glistening white table and Silas was glad when Japetus sat down right next to him, as it happened on the side facing the end of the table where the old person was sitting, and since Japetus did not touch anything but simply sat back, Silas did the same. He felt as if he were protected having Japetus there.

A moment later Ina and Jorim came running in and threw themselves upon the chair on the other side of Silas. Both of them wanted to sit there and neither would give in. Without saying a word they clawed at each other's fingers to pull them away from the chair and both tried to squeeze onto the seat, pinching each other and stepping on each other's toes.

Silas watched the fight in amazement; never before had he witnessed children fighting silently and he looked around to discover how the rest of the family was reacting. To his astonishment only Granny Nicoline had her eye on what was happening. Like a little, slightly disheveled bird, she sat deep inside her black shawl watching what was happening. Neither of the two children was able to pry the other completely away.

Then she suddenly said, "Will Ina come over here and sit next to Granny?" in a slightly hoarse but exceedingly clear voice. Silas could hear from her tone that this was a lady who was used to giving orders and being obeyed.

Ina reluctantly withdrew from the battlefield, but she had the effrontery to turn around, stick out her tongue, and make faces at her younger brother, who was rocking back and forth on the chair exultantly.

Silas stole a glance at Japetus, thinking that at least he had not been so polite and well-bred when he was born. Clearly the children of gentry were basically no different from those of ordinary people.

Last to come in, Alexander Planke took his place at the table, and after a short prayer the meal could begin. So as not to bring shame down upon himself by doing the wrong thing, Silas kept a careful eye on Japetus and imitated him: took the same things in the same order even though he might have preferred something else, drank coffee when he drank and tried terribly hard not to slurp out loud. For Silas the meal was something that simply had to be got through with as few complications as possible, so that he could be on his way.

But such was obviously not the case for the merchant and his wife, who took their time, and right in the middle of it all Alexander Planke—believe it or not—began to talk once again about how as a matter of fact he really wished he could have given Silas a horse.

Silas hurriedly swallowed what was in his mouth so that he could have a chance to protest, but the merchant anticipated him by saying he was well aware that Silas already had a horse but now they had thought of something else to give him.

No one said anything. It was obviously not considered good manners to open one's mouth before the master of the house had finished speaking, but Silas dreaded to think what gift might be inflicted on him and, in spite of the silence around the table, he interrupted Alexander Planke to say he had a wish that he really would like to have fulfilled if possible.

The merchant smiled even though he had not found the interruption in order.

Silas did not dare wait until he had finished saying everything he wanted to. "Horses do not benefit from being in the wrong hands," he began.

The smile froze on the merchant's face and gave way to mild bafflement, but Silas continued confidently. It was now or never.

"If you have horses that are as fine as the ones down in your stable, you should hire someone to look after them who has the horses' image in his heart, not someone whose mind is full of raisins and salt herring."

A deep silence settled over the table. No one was eating. Both the merchant and his wife looked at Silas with uncomprehending eyes while Japetus bit his lip and looked down at the tablecloth. Until this very moment he had been so happy and now this had destroyed it all. A stableboy, he thought, God preserve us; that was not at all what his father and mother had discussed.

"What do you mean by that?" Alexander Planke said, frowning. " 'Herring in his mind'?"

Silas put down his knife.

"I mean that your horses are much too good to be looked after by Tobias; he doesn't care about them—"

A shadow crossed the merchant's face; he thought he understood what this was leading up to.

"And so you think that we should find someone else to look after them?" he asked.

"Of course," said Silas, "that's why I said it."

"And who should that be?"

Both the merchant and his wife thought that Silas was denigrating Tobias in order to take his job away from him. Their mouths grew tight; this they had not expected.

"I don't know," said Silas, "as long as it's someone who likes it. Anyway, Tobias is much too good to be a stableboy."

"How is that?" asked Alexander Planke, not following him. "Didn't you just say that he was not good enough? How is one supposed to understand this?"

"Exactly as I said," replied Silas. "Tobias is not good for looking after horses because his head is full of butter and dried prunes and everything else you sell. He would do a much better job over in the shop, but he will never be a really good stableboy. He doesn't have the desire."

"Where did you learn this?"

"I talked with him."

"Why didn't he tell me?"

"He was afraid of being dismissed. His mother needs the money."

"And what if I do dismiss him now anyway, after what you have said?"

Silas shrugged. "Then your business would lose a

first-rate clerk. And in that case you really deserve to lose him," said Silas bluntly.

Alexander Planke concealed a wry smile behind his hand.

"And you would be able to look after my horses better than Tobias?" he asked next.

"Of course," said Silas calmly.

Alexander Planke sighed. This was not quite what he and his wife Elisabeth had thought of, but the way things developed, it might be the best solution after all. This strange boy, who had seemed so engaging and attractive the previous day, had disappointed him. It was not decent to want to take a job away from someone else.

Nevertheless he said, "It is settled then, the place is yours."

"Mine?"

Silas bolted halfway out of his chair and plopped down again.

"But I don't want any kind of job!" he exclaimed.

Japetus' head shot up.

"Didn't you just say that you could look after the horses better than Tobias?" the merchant asked almost accusingly.

"That I could," said Silas, "but I don't intend to take a job anywhere."

"Well, I don't understand any of this," sighed Alexander Planke, giving up.

Silas snatched a bite of his bread and chewed energetically, while he thought about how he could explain himself.

"You wanted to give me a horse because I caught the four-in-hand, right?"

The merchant nodded.

"Well, I don't need a horse—instead I wanted to ask you whether Tobias could be moved from the stable over to the shop. Your horses would be better off as a result—and Tobias would also have a better time, and in the end you'd benefit from both. That's all. . . . Now I'd like permission to leave."

Silas got up and shoved his chair back. But both the merchant and his wife protested vehemently, and Japetus tugged at his jacket and pressed his shoulders to make him sit down again.

"But I must," said Silas.

"Of course you will have permission to leave when you have heard what I wanted to say before. I was not finished."

Elisabeth Planke smiled expectantly.

"We just wanted to ask you whether you would like to stay here," continued Alexander Planke.

"Stay here," repeated Silas, not letting himself be pressed down into the chair again. "But I have just said that I do not want to be a stableboy, not even if Tobias is moved over to the shop; that's not why I said it."

"You shall not be a stableboy," said the merchant.

"What then?" Silas wanted to know. There was deep distrust in his voice.

"We would like to help you make something of yourself."

"What kind of something?"

"Anything—whatever you really feel like doing."

"I just want to be myself," said Silas. "I'm used to looking after myself."

"Then you could surely learn something that you

could get pleasure from," was Elisabeth Planke's opinion.

Silas thought of Ben-Godik, who had reduced himself to being a wood-carver in his village; was that the sort of something they meant?

"How old are you?" she asked before he could answer.

Silas considered, counting back.

"I must be fifteen or thereabouts," he supposed.

Since he had left Philip the sword-swallower he had not kept a very accurate reckoning of time.

"Maybe fourteen and a half," he said a little later.

"Have you ever gone to school?" the merchant wanted to know.

Silas laughed loudly in reply.

"You needn't laugh," said the merchant. "Here all the better people's children go to school."

"I am not a better person's child," laughed Silas. "I have never had time for anything like that."

"Has no one ever taught you how to read and write?"

Silas shook his head.

"I never needed to," he said.

"People who cannot read are always cheated," said the merchant.

Silas denied that. "All you have to do is use your head," he said.

"You are welcome to go to school here with the children," said Alexander Planke, "and you can go on living up in the attic and you will be given food and clothes and whatever else you need."

In saying thank you, Silas explained that it was not right for him.

"You can think it over," said the merchant.

Silas promised to do that. He was impatient to go out and look around the town before starting back, and deep inside he did not consider that this was anything to think over. He was the person he was; he saw no reason to make any changes. Food and clothing he could get for himself the way he usually did, and he would not like to give up the freedom to do what he felt like. If Japetus did not want to go out with him into the town now, then he would go off on his own.

While they walked down the stairs together, Silas thought about how they were almost the same height and almost the same age and yet as different as two people could be. Japetus was rich and educated and well-bred, he could read everything in the books in the big bookcase up in the parlor; Silas had just enough to get by but on the other hand he knew a whole lot about the practicalities of life.

Down in the entryway Carnelian went about sweeping while he whistled.

FIVE

Silas' first excursion with Japetus

NEITHER OF THE boys said very much at first. They tramped steadily down the cobbled street side by side and Silas looked around eagerly. In fact he was so busy experiencing it all that he never once noticed that various people turned around and stared after the odd pair they made. He had been in many towns over the years, but always small ones with few streets and low buildings; never had he been confronted with anything as marvelous as this. Even the town by the sea, where he had spent the previous winter with Ben-Godik and which, at the time, he had found both large and imposing, shrank by comparison and took on a rustic touch.

Not that he could have said precisely how this new town differed from all those he had seen before, but it was as if there were more of everything. Longer streets

71

and more streets, more big houses and also more small ones and, especially, lots of shops. Silas would have liked to stop at each and every one, but he could tell that this began to irritate Japetus, so he contented himself with stopping where there was something particularly remarkable to look at.

And there were so many people. It made Silas feel strange and alien; everyone was rushing hither and yon. And no one appeared to greet anyone else. Perhaps they didn't even know each other? Or else people didn't greet each other and chat awhile here the way they did elsewhere. Maybe there were simply so many people in the town that people didn't know each other at all.

The thought was overwhelming. There was something awe-inspiring about the fact that so many people could live so close together without knowing each other, and he felt deep in his soul that this was a place where a person could in fact be missing and no one would ever know it. He already no longer knew where he was in relation to the house they had left; there were far too many streets for him to be able to keep track, and they had turned so many corners that he did not even have a sense of the right direction to head back.

"How do you find out where to go in a town like this?" he asked Japetus, who was walking beside him not looking in any way oppressed by the number of streets or the density of the crowds.

"What do you mean?" asked Japetus.

"I mean, how do people tell the streets apart—how do they know when to turn a corner or when to keep going?"

"Well, after all they live here."

"Does anyone ever get lost?"

"It can happen, especially if someone ends up where there aren't any street signs. . . . Then you have to ask."

"Street signs—what are they?"

"You can see them here." Japetus drew him over to the nearest corner and pointed up on the wall of the house where there were two small wooden plaques.

"What are they for?" asked Silas.

"To tell the streets apart."

"But they're the same," objected Silas. "They all have the same colors."

"Different words are written on each one," said Japetus. "Each street has a name of its own."

"So then people read where to go?"

"No, you read the name of the street and see if it's the right one."

"What if it isn't?"

"Then you can ask someone."

Now Silas could also clearly see that the signs were not exactly the same and not equally long, but this did not really help a person who couldn't read.

Japetus turned into another street from which they emerged into a big square bustling with people and booths and stalls and pushcarts.

"But there's a market here!" Silas exclaimed, astonished that no one had mentioned it.

"No, it's just market day in the square," said Japetus. "It happens here twice a week." He pushed his way past people transacting business without taking time to see what they were buying and selling, and almost lost Silas in the confusion, since Silas stopped every time something caught his attention. He was so busy looking that he didn't notice where they were going until Japetus stopped at the foot of an immeasurably broad flight of stairs.

"What is this?" asked Silas, tilting his head back and looking up at the tallest building he had ever seen. High, high up it formed a point like a church.

"Is it a church?" he asked before Japetus could answer his first question.

"This is our cathedral," said Japetus. And Silas noticed immediately that his voice had turned solemn.

"Are you going in there?" he asked when Japetus started up the steps.

"Yes," said Japetus.

"Then I'll wait for you out here," said Silas.

"You're to come along."

"Why?"

"Don't you want to see the inside of the cathedral?"

"Can I?"

Silas did not recall his few church visits with much pleasure and he didn't like sitting still and listening to the priest condemn all the bad ways that people had of living their lives. So much of what was said always applied to him, but for all that, he did not feel he lived wrong. However, he never could get anywhere explaining this to the priest, which was why he stayed away instead. He saw no point in Japetus taking him along to something like that; he thought it was a waste of time.

"There's no service now," said Japetus, noticing his hesitation.

Silas had never been inside a church except for a service and, quite simply, it had never occurred to him that he could.

74

"We'll just go in and have a look around," said Japetus.

Silas swept the hair from his forehead and followed him into the high-ceilinged, columned space. Inside the door he stopped, overwhelmed.

Japetus turned and looked at him triumphantly, but Silas had eyes only for the building. High up, the sides closed in together to form a roof; the columns ran upward like enormous tree trunks with spreading branches, stone branches that held the roof in place. Silas didn't even dare whisper. What if the whole thing were to tumble down; he wanted to leave immediately in case it did. But Japetus went on into the building away from the safety of the door, and whatever Silas might or might not have wanted to do, he had to go along. On soundless soft shoes he stayed close behind him, convinced it could not be true that boys could just walk right in off the street—at least not boys of his sort—perhaps those like Japetus could. If an irate church sexton should happen to appear suddenly, he didn't know what to say in his defense.

Japetus scooted into a bench way up in the front, and Silas knew no better than to sit down beside him, all the time keeping his eyes peeled in case something should start to come loose up in the roof. It was simply unbelievable that it could all go on hanging up there by itself. But gradually, as nothing happened, his eyes began to seek out other points of splendor—high stained-glass windows, carved and painted figures on the altar and all around the pulpit. Under other circumstances he would have liked to have plenty of time to look at all these but his fear of being in the wrong and his fear of unforeseeable happenings were always in his mind, preventing him from giving himself fully to the sights. He saw it all and yet he did not see it: his senses sniffed catastrophe. He consumed it all, stuffed himself until his eyes were about to burst, all the time prepared to dash out if disaster should strike. The big, cold church space was a power in itself, and yet Japetus sat completely still as if waiting for something—or as if he were listening. He didn't seem frightened.

Silas listened too. Thinking that he heard a faint rustle and moan, he turned his head but could see no one who seemed in need, only an old lady with a basket on her arm who had come in from the square and sat down way in the back. She looked rather tired, but her presence comforted Silas, as it meant that other people chose to go in there too.

Suddenly the room was filled with a tremendous sound.

Silas let out a terrified yell and sprang halfway out of the pew before Japetus grabbed his arm and pulled him back with all his might.

"Hadn't we better get out quickly? Shouldn't we hurry?" Silas turned to the other boy to free himself. Surely Japetus realized that something was wrong.

But Japetus appeared to be enjoying himself immensely. There was a grin all over his face as if he had produced that mighty sound himself to play a trick on Silas. Meanwhile the sound had swelled into the space and turned into music, bigger and more all-embracing music than Silas had ever heard; he sank back down onto the bench in a state of paralysis. There were flutes.

The whole church sounded of flutes, lots of flutes all at once. The sounds came out of all the corners and he could hear migrating birds over turbulent woodlands and the thunder of surf from distant shores. It pressed him down onto the bench at the same time as it carried him along with it, and he no longer noticed Japetus or the grip on his arm as the boy kept hold of him; he only felt himself being expanded to become the church space itself, so that he had the whole of it inside himself: the columns, the vaulted ceiling, and all the statues. He became the building. And it was the building that was making the music.

Afterward he had no sense of how long it had lasted. The music stopped and Silas found himself sitting on the bench once more and in a daze he followed Japetus out into the sun and the bustling din of the square. Silent. Words would not suffice to describe how he felt, and he staggered about as if his feet were not his own.

"That was Fabian Fedder," Japetus informed him.

"What?" mumbled Silas, not hearing. His whole head still bulged with the vast music.

Japetus repeated that it had been Fabian Fedder, and Silas looked around in confusion while they descended the stone steps. He saw no one who could be the man Japetus mentioned.

"Where?" asked Silas.

"Playing, of course. He had to practice."

Silas kept quiet. He understood nothing that Japetus said. They had been inside a church where there had been no one else except an old woman, and the church had played music around them, over them, and right through them, so that Silas was not quite himself yet. That was the way it had been.

Japetus took a different street than the one they had come on, but Silas was much too preoccupied with what had happened to notice where he was going.

"That was our tutor," explained Japetus as they walked.

"Where?" asked Silas. "Who?"

"Fabian Fedder, of course."

Silas did not understand what that had to do with the church, but now he kept his mouth shut. Inside his head the music was still playing and he walked down the street with Japetus as if he were asleep, assuming that now they were on their way back.

But then quite suddenly there was water right in front of them. Not an ocean but what had to be a fairly wide river with a quay on the town side where large ships interspersed with small ones were docked. In his befuddled state Silas had not noticed that distinctive smell which otherwise always told him that he was approaching water. In a flash he felt transported back to the town by the sea where he had lived for a long time the previous winter. But this was a different kind of harbor with different types of ships. He stood still, recalling what the other town had been like, with its sturdy seafaring vessels. Here they were all of a different design: low, broad, and chunky—probably incredibly roomy—riverboats that led a cozy, sheltered life far inland and never had to withstand storms and rough seas.

Japetus waited politely until Silas had finished looking; for him the quay crowded with heavily loaded tubs and barges was a very ordinary sight, but he realized that it might surprise someone who was not used to it.

Something was happening all the time. There were ships taking on barrels and others from which barrels were being rolled ashore; there were ships carrying wood and ships with vegetables and some with grain in gray sacks and, mixed in among them, some that appeared to be empty. But common to them all was the fact that people were living on board.

Not sailors like those he had seen on the seagoing ships, but men with wives and children and dogs and cats and, here and there, cages with chickens. Laundry was hung out to dry; people were shouting that food was ready just as in real houses. In one place he saw a pig with a rope around its neck tied to a gunwale and somewhere else it was a small child that was tethered and everywhere there was play and talk and shouting and crying and peeing into the water, while cargo was being unloaded and new goods carried on board.

Silas tried to imagine what being on these floating houses would be like. In some places ships were moored next to each other, stacked two or three deep at the quayside, so that people from the ships farthest out had to cross over the others to get land under their feet. He began to walk down the quay with Japetus behind him. He thought about how slowly some of the barges probably moved. Going one way, they could just let themselves be carried along by the current, the other way they would have to be pulled by horses walking patiently along the riverbank. To him, used to riding around on horseback with the wind whistling through his clothes, this life seemed far too quiet. Perhaps not exactly as secure as living in a house, but on the other hand it was not what he could picture for himself. No real speed could be got out of it.

Japetus explained what kind of ships there were, where they came from, and what they carried, but Silas listened with only half an ear; he was more preoccupied with what to him was an unfamiliar way of life. He stared at the people; time and again he turned to look at the town from their perspective. And in the back of his head the music was still playing, although he wasn't really thinking about it.

Once he had come drifting downstream, but that river had been smaller and narrower; that boat had been quite small and not the kind a person could live on. Worn out by hunger, indifferent to where he was going, he had lain in the hull with his feet up over the gunwale trying to drown out his grumbling stomach by playing his flute. High and low riverbank cliffs, isolated houses, and tiny villages had sailed past, but never had he come to a place like this though he still wondered whether that little river might have joined this bigger one and whether he would have got here if he had endured his hunger somewhat longer and had not gone ashore at Bartolin the horse trader's place.

But then he would never have got the black mare— Japetus tugged his arm and interrupted his thoughts. "We have to go home now."

Silas pulled himself together, remembering that after all he was living in the merchant's house. He had almost forgotten the overwhelming experience of the previous day. There was bound to be a good deal more to be seen here, and he decided on the spot to stay with the Plankes for a few days, perhaps a whole week, before heading home.

There was already far too much that he wanted to have a better look at and he was sure that more would turn up.

They walked slowly back along the quay.

"This is where we get our goods," explained Japetus. Silas nodded. He could see that.

"If we ask Father, I'm sure we can get permission to go down into some of the ships," continued Japetus. "That is, if you would like to see inside them."

"Can't we do that now before we go?" asked Silas.

The other boy shook his head.

"Not really," he said. "We have to ask permission first."

"So they're your father's ships?" Silas wanted to know.

"No," said Japetus.

"Then we can just ask someone who lives on board."

Japetus shuddered at the thought.

"Do you always do exactly what comes into your head?" he asked.

"Yes, if I feel like it. . . . After all, I have no father," he added by way of explanation.

"But your mother," said Japetus. "Or that man Philip? Or some other adult?"

Silas grinned. Japetus didn't understand how some-one no older than himself could be so confident about life without having a single person to lean on.

"No one tells me what to do," said Silas, "but of

81

course that means I have to fend for myself if I get into hot water. You just have to keep your head up and think fast."

He thought it must be incredibly boring to have other people decide everything for you.

"Can't you decide anything at all for yourself?" he asked.

"I almost always get permission to do what I ask for," Japetus replied.

Silas shrugged; that did not sound particularly heartening to him. They walked awhile side by side in silence.

"What would you do if your father ordered you to learn to swallow swords?" Silas asked suddenly. He really wanted to know how Japetus would react to the situation that had made him go out into the world on his own.

"Swords?"

Japetus stopped so abruptly that a baker's boy with a basket ran into him from behind.

"What swords?"

He turned to Silas in astonishment, paying no attention to the baker's boy who was cursing under his breath because he had almost dropped what he was carrying.

"If he told you that you had to learn to be a sword-swallower," explained Silas.

"Well, he wouldn't. Why should he do that? I'm supposed to learn how to manage the business."

"But if he did order you—what would you do?"

Japetus looked at him uncomprehendingly.

It was, in fact, a crazy question, thought Silas. No one would ever dream of making Japetus become a sword-swallower. But that was not really what Silas wanted to measure as much as the extent of his obedience.

"Move yourself, goddamn money bags," snarled the baker's boy from behind.

"Go around," said Silas. "There's plenty of room."

"I have to go down to the ship," said the baker's boy.

"Oh," said Silas, lifting the big white dish towel covering the basket. "Will you give me one?" he asked, catching sight of the golden rolls.

Without waiting for a reply he grabbed a roll from the basket.

"No," said Japetus, taking his wrist. "Don't do that."

Silas was so startled that he dropped the roll. The baker's boy dodged past them and away, laughing scornfully.

"Why?" asked Silas.

"One shouldn't start a conversation with them," said Japetus gravely.

"With whom?"

Japetus jerked his head in the direction of the baker's boy, who was on his way down to one of the barges with the basket.

"But he was really fresh," objected Silas. "He needed to be shown a thing or two."

"That doesn't matter. You should pretend that it was nothing."

"Why do that?" Silas asked again.

"It isn't good manners to start a quarrel with common people on the street," said Japetus. "One should not have anything to do with them—"

Silas chewed on this awhile.

"What about me?" he asked.

Japetus turned his head slightly and said, "There's something different about you."

"But I suppose I'm 'common' too." Silas' voice became aggressive. "Maybe you feel you have to hang around with me because I happened to save you from being smashed into a tree yesterday, right?"

"No, there's something different about you," repeated Japetus, uneasy about this turn the conversation had taken.

"Maybe you think the baker's boy would swallow swords if he was told to," Silas asked.

Japetus couldn't help noticing the sarcasm. Silas felt that it would really be good for the rich man's son to get out and sample a little of the common life. On the other hand, it certainly wasn't his fault that he was the way he was.

Over by one of the barges a wagon stopped and Silas recognized Carnelian on the box.

"Oh good! There's the one with water in the streets!" he exclaimed happily.

Japetus looked at him as if he had suddenly gone insane. But Silas laughed and pointed to the wagon.

"That's Carnelian," said Japetus.

"Exactly!" said Silas.

"Why did you say he has water in the streets?"

"He sounds like it; can't you hear that yourself?" He walked over to the wagon in which there were two barrels of salted herring.

"Could we ride home with you?" he asked.

Horrified, Japetus tugged at his arm. "This is a work wagon," he murmured, advising Silas against it.

"It certainly is a fine one," said Silas, "with only two barrels so there's plenty of room for us." He ignored Japetus' protests nonchalantly, and looked questioningly at the driver, who, for his part, glanced from one boy to the other.

"Can we?" asked Silas again.

Carnelian met his subtle look and realized what he was up to; there was a flash of humor in his eye. They shared secrets and now the merchant's son was going to get in and ride with the herring.

"Now I wonder about that," murmured the driver, but since Silas was already up in the back of the wagon, Japetus had to go along if only to save face.

SIX

A partial change

"WELL," SAID ELISABETH Planke when they arrived home, "have you decided whether you will stay with us?"

"Yes," said Silas, noticing how anxiously she waited for him to continue. She really did seem to want him to stay.

"I would like to stay here," he said guardedly.

"Oh, that's wonderful!" she smiled happily, "but I thought as much. . . . And you may be sure that you will not regret it," she added.

"A while anyway," said Silas quietly, trying to moderate her enthusiasm somewhat. He could not abide the way she had said that. It sounded as if she had a plan for him, as if she expected to stake out a new future for him.

"For his own good," Silas added to himself.

"What do you mean by 'a while'?" she asked attentively, assuming that he probably meant a year or so.

"A week," said Silas.

"A week!" repeated Elisabeth Planke, aghast. The joy in her face extinguished before his very eyes. "Why only a week?" she asked, disappointed.

"I have to go home to Ben-Godik," explained Silas. "He has no idea where I am."

This was not the whole truth, but Silas avoided saying more. In any event she would not be able to understand his aversion to being confined.

"Then you'll return when you've told him where you are?" asked the merchant's wife hopefully.

That was a possibility Silas had not envisaged and at first he did not know what to reply.

Finally he said, "I don't know," thus avoiding promising anything.

"You probably never decide what you are going to do such a long time in advance," the mistress queried.

"No," admitted Silas, he certainly did not; he took things as they came up.

"Well then we must at least make the most of the week you will be here," continued the merchant's wife optimistically.

With slight displeasure, Silas immediately detected a new decisiveness in her tone of voice. Now, he thought, she will really try to make this week so "good" that I'll feel like staying on in their house.

She did not wait for an answer, but patted his hair lightly. "Now go up to your room and wash before lunch. Clean clothes have been laid out on your bed," she said, turning to go.

"Japetus is tidying up now," she added, since he did not move. Then she left, and Silas remained staring dumbly at the door to the dim little passage leading to their residence.

What did she say? Clean clothes? But he had no clean clothes; why would he need any? He stared down at his good sheepskin coat, new from last winter. What did she mean? He was wearing his clothes.

Slowly he turned and left the kitchen, where Anna was bossing and bullying the pots and pans. For a second the thought wandered through his mind that he could ask her what the mistress had meant. But Anna did not look as if she had heard anything out of the ordinary, so he gave up and decided instead to go to his room and wash his face and hands and maybe comb his hair, so that at least they could see his good intentions. Clean clothes were not something he could easily come by— nor did he want to.

Just as he opened the door to the little room where he had spent the night, Silas thought that he had made a mistake. His bed looked as if no one had slept in it, and on top of the bedcover a whole array of strange clothes was neatly displayed. He had to go back out into the corridor and count the doors before he was sure. Then he walked in hesitantly and closed the door behind him.

Had they given the room to someone else while he was out?

But hadn't the mistress said "his room"?

She had also said something about clean clothes on

his bed, he suddenly remembered, so then he was not supposed to get them himself. He walked swiftly over to the bed and unfolded the neatly arranged articles of clothing one by one.

Knee breeches. . . . And stockings. . . . And a shirt like the one Japetus was wearing, and a waistcoat, and a colored scarf to tie around his neck. . . . And on the floor a pair of shoes with shiny buckles.

Am I supposed to wear all this? thought Silas in a daze, starting to grope his way out of his own clothes without taking his eyes off what was lying on the bed. These must belong to Japetus.

Something white was lying there too. It had to be something to wear underneath. Silas held it up in front of him, he had never worn anything like it before— what a bother all these different pieces were anyway, what a lot of time it must take whenever you had to put them all on or take them off. He walked over to the wash-stand and poured out some water. He had better give the back of his neck a going over too, so that not too much would rub off on this finery.

Afterward, when he had pulled on the strange clothes, he stood awhile looking at his own things. Now his clothes were lying on the bed, and it was as if he saw them in a completely different light. His farmer's coat looked just the way those coats always do after they have been worn a certain amount of time, and his trousers had little in common with the ones he was wearing now: His were full of holes and frayed and they ended vaguely somewhere on the small of the leg. What is more, he also had to admit that they looked a little shabby. But still the greatest change was the shoes. His soft leather shoes were on the floor now, half under the bed, while his feet were rigidly squeezed into the new ones with buckles. Cautiously Silas took a couple of steps across the floor to accustom himself to the feeling, and he could not help lifting his feet a little higher than he did in his soft leather shoes which fitted like part of himself. Now it was as if he were walking in deep snow. And what a racket they made! Silas was not used to people being able to hear him move.

Then he combed his hair with the last drop of water and started on his way downstairs, holding onto the banister all the way so as not to trip in the strange shoes. It was as if someone quite different were walking down the stairs. The hard soles of the shoes made an echo like wooden clogs, and the trousers pinched around his knees in a peculiar, unfamiliar way, and he found the kerchief around his neck equally uncomfortable because it prevented him from seeing where he was stepping. He was altogether unused to noticing his clothes; they usually went along with him naturally like part of his body.

Down in the kitchen Anna studied him with a swift sidelong glance while she lifted lids and stirred pots. But since she made no remarks Silas assumed that he looked the way he should now and he went on into the parlor.

In there Elisabeth Planke rose with an exclamation of pleasure and came over and took Silas by the shoulders and turned him around so that she could see him from all sides.

"Fine—fine," she said, turning him this way and that.

Silas was quite aware that she was satisfied by his appearance even though the way he felt was definitely

91

not "fine" but more accurately oppressed by the borrowed clothes.

"He looks exactly like Japetus now," said Jorim, planting himself unceremoniously right in front of Silas and casting his eyes up and down the unrecognizably altered boy.

"He looks like Japetus all over except for his hair," added Ina, who was sitting on the sofa with a book in her lap.

"Yes," said her mother quietly. There was something about the way she said it which led Silas to suspect that this wretched matter would soon be remedied. She would stamp out this difference as well. Involuntarily Silas touched his damp, recently combed hair which reached down to his shoulders. Alexander Planke's son's hair only touched his ear lobes.

The merchant's wife did not let go of Silas' arm but drew him over to a big oval mirror which hung between the windows.

"Look," she said proudly as if she herself had created both the boy and the clothes single-handedly.

Silas gave a start at the sight of the unknown boy in the mirror staring out at him with his own eyes.

"Is that me?" he asked, instantly aware what a stupid question that was, because it was obviously he. He could see that perfectly well.

From the dining room Thea announced that the meal was now on the table, and with a broad gesture Elisabeth Planke swept Silas and the two smaller children before her toward the door. This time there was no possible way for Silas to slip out to the kitchen. The delicate, proud lady had taken matters into her own hands summarily, making choices for him just as she did for Japetus and his siblings. Silas had said that he would stay with them for a week, but he had apparently said yes to more than merely living at their house: He had to follow the customs of the house while he was there.

Japetus rushed in from a door at the opposite end of the dining room, stopping abruptly at the sight of this new edition of Silas. He had not heard his mother say that clean clothes had been laid out for the guest; he was completely unprepared for the boy's altered appearance. And somehow it looked as if he were disappointed. Silas, who was particularly sensitive because of not being used to the situation, noticed this right away.

"Don't you think Silas looks splendid now?" his mother asked, smiling.

"Yes," said Japetus dutifully, going over to his place at the table. He did not sound enthusiastic.

"You have to tell me what to use," said Silas, indicating the countless knives and forks and spoons laid out at his place.

With a strangely closed expression Japetus promised that he would, and Silas wondered whether this might be because of his clothes, because Japetus' mother had taken them and given them away without his having agreed to it. He certainly had not been like this in the morning. Silas decided to find out the reason, but that had to wait; right now he had more than enough to do finding out how to eat.

No sooner had the dessert been dispatched and thanks been expressed, than he drew Japetus with him under the pretext of going down to the stable to attend to his horse. . . . And of course he did have to do that, but he mostly went to find out what had happened to the merchant's son's good spirits.

Japetus tried to wriggle out of it.

"There's nothing wrong," he maintained.

"Yes, there is," Silas went on. "And if it's because your mother has given me some of your clothes, you just tell me and I'll change back into my own."

Japetus sighed.

"It isn't the clothes," he said. "I have plenty of clothes."

"Then what is it?"

They were walking slowly down the stairs next to each other.

"It's because now you look like all the other boys I know," came the sad remark from Japetus. "Now you are just as neat and rich and—and boring."

Silas laughed out loud with relief.

"Go right ahead and laugh," said Japetus darkly, "but I liked you better the way you were before."

"Do you think I'll become different because I'm wearing other clothes?" laughed Silas.

"If you wear them long enough, you will," said Japetus. "At least you will if you are going to stay here in this house."

"Not in a week," said Silas.

Japetus said nothing.

"Anyway, you're wrong," said Silas, turning serious. "I won't change because of wearing your trousers; I won't end up being like you at all because of that— except perhaps in a mirror—but that's not what you meant, is it? No one can change me."

Japetus looked at him skeptically.

"You don't know Mother," he said gloomily.

"No," admitted Silas, "indeed I don't—but then she doesn't know me either."

A faint smile appeared on Japetus' face.

"I rather think there's a danger I might have a bad influence on her well-brought-up son," continued Silas. "I'm not at all sure that she'll care to keep me in the long run."

Silas let his hands slide down the banister and took the last big section of the stairs in one jump. The stiff, hard shoes made him land with a thud in front of the door to the shop.

"Hush," said Japetus involuntarily.

Silas laughed again.

"There, you can see for yourself," he said. "I behave like a wild creature even in your shoes."

"Father detests noise," explained Japetus.

"Well, so do I," said Silas, "when others make it."

They went out into the courtyard.

"Still, I wouldn't mind learning a few things," continued Silas on their way to the stable.

"What do you mean?" asked Japetus.

"For example, it's bothersome not to be able to read street signs in a city, I think—and not to know the right thing to do at the dinner table in good company."

Japetus sighed; he was listening with only half an ear. It had been so marvelous when this strange boy came riding right out of the blue and stopped his father's runaway horses. He had seemed so much stronger to Japetus because he represented an entirely different way of life and everything about him was different—but now his mother had already begun to bend what was marvelous to suit the custom in better people's homes. . . . It had never occurred to him that a boy his own age could be completely responsible for making all the choices in his own life. He only knew children who were characterized as polite or impolite depending on how totally their behavior conformed to their parents' wishes.

"Couldn't we work it out so that you get something from me and I get something from you in exchange?" Silas interrupted his train of thought.

"How do you mean?" asked Japetus.

"You teach me how a person lives who is the son of the town's richest merchant and in return I teach you how to get along if you aren't that."

"How in the world would you do it?" Japetus exclaimed in surprise.

"I really don't know yet—but you'll probably end up quarreling with both your father and mother. They'll definitely regret taking me in—but you'll benefit from it."

"How will you manage it all in a week?" asked Japetus hopefully.

"I'm bound to be chucked out before then," prophesied Silas cheerily. "And your father will be angry at you."

"I'll still do what you say," promised Japetus.

"Wrong," said Silas immediately. "You've got it all wrong. I'm not the one to say what you should or shouldn't do: you have to decide that for yourself without having an eye out for what your father or I think—and you have to take full responsibility for what you decide."

This was a whole new idea to Japetus and he stood quietly for a long time while Silas made sure that the mare had everything she needed.

Then Silas said, "Actually, I feel like taking a ride."

"I would really like to do that too," said Japetus longingly. But Silas could hear from his despondent tone that he had already given up in advance.

"Why don't you?" asked Silas.

"I always have to ask whether I may borrow a horse and Father is sleeping now—besides, I have to go to school in an hour."

"To school!" exclaimed Silas.

"Our tutor is coming soon."

Silas looked at him appraisingly.

"Well, you have to decide that for yourself," he said calmly, starting to put the bridle on the mare.

Japetus writhed with inward pain. There was not the slightest doubt that he would much prefer taking a ride with Silas, but the thought of how he could explain his absence to his parents and the tutor nagged at him.

"What should I tell them?" he moaned.

"That you felt more like taking a ride with me, of course. What else?"

Japetus stared at Silas as if he had never seen him before. It had never occurred to him that it could be so simple.

"But I can't ride in these clothes either," he added.

"Oh," said Silas.

"And you can't either," continued Japetus.

"Oh really?" said Silas grinning. "Maybe I have to go to school too."

"That I don't know," mumbled Japetus, but Silas could hear behind the words that this had indeed been the idea.

"Which one do you usually ride?" Silas asked, to end the discussion.

"It varies, depending on which needs exercise."

Silas let his glance roam over the numerous horses in the stable; there were both heavier cart horses and lighter saddle horses.

Then he asked, "Which one do you like best?"

"The dapple," said Japetus without hesitation, pointing to a dappled gelding at the back of the stable.

"Then saddle him up," ordered Silas.

"I never do that myself," the other apologized.

"Then let Tobias do it."

"He's eating over in the servants' kitchen with Carnelian and the shop assistant."

"Shall I show you how to do it?" offered Silas.

Japetus scraped the floor self-consciously with the tip of his shoe and Silas realized that he was angry with himself because he had to admit that he couldn't do it himself.

"After all, you showed me which fork to use," Silas added. The other boy merely nodded. Silas went into the tack room and chose a saddle and a blanket to put under it. The dapple turned his head and sniffed at Silas inquisitively but otherwise let himself be covered with the saddle and a bridle. And Silas constantly made sure that Japetus was following what was happening so that he could do it himself the next time.

The mare was ready as she was, for Silas owned

neither a saddle nor a saddle blanket—he sat right on her shiny black coat. The horse rested her head lovingly on his shoulder while he untied her.

"That's that," said Silas, opening the stable door.

Japetus led the dapple out into the yard, glancing around uneasily. He had never taken a horse from the stable without first asking permission and without reporting beforehand where he intended to go. He stole a glance at Silas, who was carefully closing the stable door behind him. What might happen if his father were suddenly to appear was impossible to predict, but he hoped that nothing would happen until they had got well and truly away from there. After that, it was all the same to him.

Out through the entry dashed Tobias, holding a big piece of sausage speared on his fork, his eyes round with alarm, having heard the sound of horses' hoofs. Had the master given an order that he had not heard?

"Has the master given word for horses to be saddled?" he whispered anxiously.

"No," said Silas. "You just finish eating."

"What's happening?"

In his mind's eye the stableboy already pictured his future in the shop going up in smoke because of an order that had not been carried out.

"They need to be exercised, that's all," said Silas.

"Who said so?" asked Tobias, confused.

He had never known of a horse being saddled without him.

"Japetus," answered Silas calmly, moving past the gaping boy who was standing stiffly holding the forked sausage, which in his haste he had forgotten to put down.

"But—" said Tobias.

"No buts, we're taking a ride."

And with no further talk the two boys mounted and disappeared down the street. Not until they could no longer be seen did Tobias remember the sausage and hurry in to see what had become of his cabbage.

SEVEN

Silas' second excursion with Japetus

"WHERE SHALL WE go?" asked Silas, looking around.

"Where do you think?"

"Well, there really isn't too much choice," Silas stated.

Japetus looked at him in astonishment. For his part, he felt that the whole world stretched open before him now that he had actually managed to escape from his ancestral home. How could this fellow say that there wasn't much to choose from? He asked for an explanation.

"Down there is the river," explained Silas patiently. "That way we won't get far—and in the opposite direction there is really not too much to see: I came from there. So the choice that's left is whether we should ride up along the river or down. Which way do you know best?"

"We usually ride upstream. Many people we know have houses with big estates out along the river that way, and there are bridle paths to follow, so everyone rides that way. . . . It's also the quickest way out of town."

"That sounds good," said Silas. "Let's ride downstream."

"Do you really want to?"

"Don't you?" Silas asked in reply.

Japetus shook his head.

"It's not a nice place," he said. "All the old quays are there and you don't get out into open country."

"That doesn't matter," said Silas. "I'd like to see that part too."

"But there are so many taverns and sordid drinking places and always a lot of drunken people looking for a fight and things like that. You shouldn't go there if you don't belong. You'll be attacked."

"Have you ever been there?" asked Silas with interest.

Japetus shook his head.

"Then how do you know all this?"

"It's what I've heard. You hear lots of stories about people who were lost in the old parts of town and got into trouble."

"It sounds promising," said Silas. "I think we should ride down there and see if it's true."

Japetus hesitated.

"Remember what we agreed," said Silas. "You don't have to come along; you make your own decisions. I just want to see if it's true that people are worse there than anywhere else."

He turned the corner into one of the small alleys leading down to the river. Japetus followed reluctantly, not knowing what else to do, and seconds later they came out onto a quay of a somewhat older appearance than the one they had inspected that morning. Here, too, a number of vessels were docked, but here there was no activity; unlike the first place no one was loading or unloading; the sun was shining quietly down upon the neglected quay. The old tubs did not look all that seaworthy either; a couple of them even appeared on the verge of sinking, and as if to demonstrate the possibility, parts of ships stuck up out of the water here and there. Everything was humble and old and very poor.

Japetus shuddered.

"Anyway, it's very peaceful here," said Silas, riding out into the open stretch between the row of houses and the moored boats. A couple of old women with gray wispy hair and gray slippers on their feet caught sight of them and bustled away. A flock of dirty children stared at them from a safe place between the hovels, and from behind unclean windows in the small taverns various bearded faces turned to follow their progress.

"Where do we get to if we go on?" asked Silas.

"I don't know. I don't like being here," said Japetus.

"But no one is doing anything to us."

"They stare so," said Japetus.

"Does that hurt you?"

"I think it's an unsavory, vulgar neighborhood," Japetus continued.

"It certainly is that," replied Silas. "Most of the people who live here would probably prefer to live somewhere else but they can't afford to."

"Afford?" asked Japetus. "They could certainly work like everyone else."

Silas grunted.

"Do you think your father would employ anyone from here? A new stableboy, for example?"

"No," admitted Japetus. "But after all they could work somewhere else."

"Where?"

Japetus fell silent. He had never thought about the people there like this before.

Silas said nothing either but rode right out onto the half-rotten quay and looked into the barges inquisitively. He could see that people were living in most of them but not as many families with children as where he had been that morning. These were not decent, upstanding folk earning an honest living but decidedly shady characters who kept clear of the better citizenry of the town.

Silas continued rather slowly down along the row of small, ramshackle vessels—until suddenly the black mare would not go any further. Silas prodded her flanks encouragingly with the heels of his new shoes, and when that did not help he patted her neck comfortingly. There must be something she disliked, perhaps a scent that frightened her. Whatever, there was nothing in sight that could be the cause.

Silas inhaled but smelled nothing other than old fish and foul river water and he tried once more to urge the black on. She turned her head to one side and laid back her ears with every sign of displeasure. When Silas turned to see how the dapple was, he saw that it was behaving the same way. There had to be something they could perceive but the boys could not. Japetus had a tough job preventing his horse from galloping back the way they had come.

Silas turned around and rode over to him. Japetus was just as wildly disturbed by the place as the horses were; he too was convinced that something had frightened them which he and Silas could not see.

"What do you think it is?" he asked in a low voice.

"I don't know," said Silas, "but it must be a smell." He sniffed but noticed nothing unusual.

"Perhaps fire," suggested Japetus. "There might be a fire somewhere."

"But it doesn't smell of fire here at all," protested Silas, once again drawing a sizable snort of the quay's air down into his lungs. "It must be something else."

"Hadn't we better turn around?" asked Japetus.

"Why? No one is doing anything to us."

"The horses might go crazy. They might bolt."

Since the ride with the runaway four-in-hand, Japetus had developed a powerful respect for frightened horses.

"There are lots of other places we can ride," he said urgently.

"Yes," said Silas, but it did not sound as if he had taken in what the boy said, because he was already dismounting, determined to investigate the matter more closely. His curiosity had always been greater than his fear of the unknown, and now was no exception. He handed his reins to Japetus and told him to take the two horses back off the quay until they calmed down and to wait there.

Japetus tried to protest, but Silas had already left. He headed for the barge that had caused the mare to balk and shy away. Something strange must be on board. The black mare's instinct had never been wrong, and since Silas would rather know everything that he possibly could, he wanted to investigate the matter immediately on his own account before they went on. You never know when you can use what you find out.

He walked as quietly as he could in his new shoes, thinking that this kind of shoe was not really very practical. Not only did they make a noise so that one and all could hear where he was, but they were also without a doubt hopeless should he suddenly have to take to his heels. The soles were both slippery and stiff compared with the soft leather ones that he was used to. But of course these were upper class—with buckles.

He stopped right next to the ship and took a deep breath, but the mixture of fish that had been too long on land, boiled cabbage, and rotting garbage was all he inhaled. There were no unusual sounds nor was anything moving on any of the other barges, although Silas had the distinct impression that they were lived in. This was not a row of empty, dead riverboats; they were being used, though they no longer sailed. As far as most of them were concerned, quite a long time had passed since they could be used for river transport, but they had not stopped being the haunt of people with no other place to live.

As silently as possible Silas slipped over the gunwale and onto the deck. Still nothing moved, there were no sounds to be heard except for the big town's daytime drone, which hardly reached this part by the river. The only other sound came from small wavelets splashing against the rotting sides of the ships.

In the middle of the deck the square black hole of a hatch yawned into the belly of the barge.

From land Japetus saw Silas disappear completely from sight when he went on board and this automatically made him feel anxious. All too often he had been told terrifying tales about the kind of people who lived there: all the outcasts who could not stay anywhere else, thieves and brigands and people with contagious diseases, Gypsies and bad women and people with severely deformed bodies—all those who could not be tolerated by decent families. Japetus couldn't understand why Silas wanted to be there at all. He did not share Silas' curiosity to know what took place beyond the narrow confines of his own existence. Why couldn't they have ridden somewhere else just as well, somewhere nice, where they didn't have to be frightened of anything? He craned his neck to see what had become of Silas.

Silas was still hanging over the hatch casing with his hair like a tuft of river grass down in the hole. A ladder went down one side of the casing, and a square patch of light showed how far down it was to the bottom; the rest was thick, impenetrable darkness to a pair of eyes up in the daylight.

A snort issued from the darkness.

He got up for a moment to check where Japetus and the horses were in relation to him, and Japetus took advantage of the occasion to beckon with one arm. He did not want to stay there any longer.

Silas shook his head so that his hair swept around his ears—something about all this fascinated him. The far-off snort from the depths of the half-rotten vessel sounded as if more than one were snorting. But what attracted his attention most strongly was the smell.

Not all the time, but occasionally, a waft drifted up that was not directly connected with the surroundings. The smell was totally unlike anything around there.

Instead of returning Japetus' wave, Silas stuck his head back down into the hatch. Something about that smell reminded him of something, if only he could remember where he had encountered it before.

All around him the sun burned down on the deck; the darkened deck planks welcomed the sun's heat and although he had a direct view of one part of the city, he still felt pleasantly cut off from it. The gurgling water supplied a sensation of peace and seclusion and if a person wanted to increase that retirement from the world he could cast off and sail away—as long as the tub was in shape to stay afloat.

Silas began to understand why people lived on ships.

But that was not why he was there. He wanted to know what was down in the big black darkness under the deck. So, stretching himself flat on his stomach, he took out his flute, and with his head and both arms out over the edge of the hatch, he played a cheerful, almost wild melody.

The result did not fail to occur. A sudden tumult and fumbling around began under the deck; howls and curses about being stepped on mingled with the sounds of objects being overturned while a ponderous creature approached the ladder.

Silas stared down in suspense, ready to dash away, but

at the same time he played gently and compellingly to quiet the agitated tempers down inside the barge. It was certainly not his intention to get on the wrong side of anyone. Peace and friendliness filtered softly from the flute and spread over the ship. Somewhere on the quay Japetus was waiting, he knew.

Down at the foot of the ladder two green eyes shone in the darkness. It was an animal, and a big one at that. Silas laughed to himself; suddenly he knew why something about the smell down there had seemed familiar to him. It was a bear. That was what had frightened the horses.

But a bear cannot curse and swear—even the best-trained bear cannot learn to talk—there must be an owner down there as well.

The bear came up the ladder easily as if it had always lived there, and Silas drew back to the gunwale, still playing. Next to the hatch casing the bear, in fine fettle, rose up on its hind legs and swayed in time to the music. A piece of rope dangled from its collar and Silas could not help being reminded of the bear that he had met at the market in the town by the sea. But that town was so far away that this was not likely to be the same one. Besides, so many people traveled with bears and earned their living by making them perform.

The bear went on swaying and dancing and Silas waved to Japetus to come closer, and Japetus, who did not know what to think, quickly tethered the two horses to one of the trees on the quayside and hurried over. But when he saw what was happening on the deck he stopped as if nailed to the spot.

"Are you crazy?" he whispered in terror.

"It's a bear," explained Silas quite unnecessarily. "It's dancing."

Japetus could see that very clearly with his own eyes and he saw more than that as well, for up through the hatch stuck a head with sharp features cast in shadow by the broad brim of a black, high-crowned hat.

"Come on," said Silas invitingly.

Japetus shook his head and nodded warningly in the direction of the hatch.

Silas looked over there and a huge smile of recognition spread across his face. He was about to greet her with a cheery shout when he stopped himself. He wanted to wait awhile before saying who he was, to see whether she could recognize him, for he certainly was the one who had changed the most.

Apparently she did not recognize him. At least not yet. Her sharp, black gaze looked him over carefully while with ominous mildness she asked him what the hell he was doing there.

"Playing music," replied Silas, removing the flute from his mouth. The bear sank down on all fours and sniffed his knee.

"Who asked you to?" inquired the Horse Crone, while she glowered at the length of his well-clothed body appraisingly. And the more she stared the more Silas felt certain that he would be recognized. As always her greasy gray wisps of hair stuck out from under her hat in every direction.

She repeated the question: Who asked him to play?

"No one," said Silas.

"Then why do you do it?"

110

"Because he likes it," said Silas, pointing to the bear.

"But see here, I don't. Scram. If you think you can do anything you fancy just because your dad is filthy rich, then you're wrong."

Silas turned and looked at Japetus, who still did not dare come on board.

"Did you hear that?" he asked.

"Who is he?" asked the Horse Crone mistrustfully before Japetus was able to give a sign of life. "Your brother?"

"No, are you crazy? *His* father is the one who is filthy rich—and his father is also the one who gave us permission to come aboard."

"His father? No one here can tell me what to do, you can be sure. And no one can tell me anywhere else either."

The Horse Crone's voice lost some of its spiteful mildness and turned sharp and wrathful. Nothing offended her as deeply as the assertion that someone could decide her fate.

"Could this be your own barge?" Silas asked teasingly.

"You can swear to that, ducky. And no one can come along and tell me that I have to pay someone when the time comes to move. . . . So tell me, who's he the son of, that scaredy-cat over there?"

With a long yellow finger she pointed unceremoniously to the part of Japetus that she could see.

"Alexander Planke," said Silas without blinking and without losing sight of the Horse Crone's face. He just wanted to know whether she knew who Alexander Planke was. But there was no doubt that the name had its effect, for that whole fine figure of a woman came swiftly up onto the deck so that she could inspect Japetus in all his glory. Then she turned abruptly and stared penetratingly at Silas.

"Then who are you? If he is Planke's son, who is your father?"

"Oh, I'm just someone along with him," replied Silas evasively. He did not want to destroy the impression of the powerful merchant's name by saying that his father was no one special, but on the other hand he did not want to lie either. After all, he might be recognized any second. But now Japetus joined in the conversation.

"That isn't true!" he exclaimed. "He's almost part of our family; he's living with us."

The Horse Crone looked from one to the other.

"What kind of family?" she wanted to know. "A cousin or something?"

"Yes," said Japetus before Silas could protest.

The Horse Crone's black eyes swept searchingly over Silas' clothes again before stopping at his face, and he could see how she ransacked her memory because she could not exactly place where she had seen that face before. Then suddenly she leaned over the hatch and yelled a name down into the darkness:

"Valerian—VALERIAN!"

Judging by the intensity of the sound, it had to be either a huge man or else someone who usually slept very soundly. But then Silas thought of Jef: She had shouted for him like that too and he was only a little boy. . . . Had she managed to steal another child? But now she had no knife-grinding cart to be pulled, and she had just informed him that she sailed around.

112

Silas waited expectantly but nothing happened.

The Horse Crone shouted again. And at long last a response could be heard from the depths.

"What is it?"

"Come up here," she ordered.

Something moved around down there.

"And bring the box too," continued the Horse Crone, leaning over the edge of the hole again menacingly.

Whoever was called Valerian grumbled and protested down under the deck.

"You're wrong, it isn't time yet," observed the voice, with reluctance.

"Do as I say and spare us your nonsense," answered the former knife-grinder with undiminished vocal power. Silas noticed that Japetus started whenever she opened her mouth to send a new order down into the barge's hold. He had certainly never heard the equal of that voice before. It definitely hadn't grown any gentler with time, Silas had to admit. . . . What kind of box was she talking about? What could it be that this Valerian was supposed to bring up? A cage for the bear that was shuffling around on its own, snuffling along the gunwale? Impossible. First of all, it didn't need a cage and, second, no one person could struggle up a ladder with an object that large and sufficiently sturdy. What was it then?

But something was happening down below. The Horse Crone stuck her head over the edge and nodded in acknowledgment; she stayed right next to the hatch and Silas had to control his curiosity awhile longer. It could be a trap, he thought, remembering only too well

113

the time that this same woman wanted to throw him under the mill wheel while it was turning. There was never any way of knowing what she might dream up.

Eventually something made of shiny brown wood came into sight with a huffing and puffing from someone beneath it. Polished and fine as a piece of furniture from Elisabeth Planke's parlor. Silas had never expected that. It had decorative carvings on it too. The box swayed a little in the middle of the hole, apparently borne on the shoulder of someone who had difficulty steadying it.

"Thank you, my treasure," said the Horse Crone, lifting the contraption up onto the deck with one hand, thus revealing wheels underneath it. Narrow, thin metal wheels. The box itself was furnished with shiny fittings and had a handle on one side.

Silas had never seen an object like it before nor could he make out what kind of piece of furniture it was or what the Horse Crone would use it for. When he thought back to her house and how she had treated her few possessions, it was totally inconceivable to him that she could have something like this in her care without having somehow managed to destroy it. He stared so intently at the polished box that he almost forgot to look for the person who had brought it up into the daylight: that Valerian to whom the Horse Crone had shouted her orders. Suddenly he saw someone standing on the deck beside her who only came up to her waist.

But he was not a child: a tiny little man, no bigger than Jorim, yet surely just as old in years as the big bony woman who apparently ordered him around.

Silas no longer knew what to expect, but at least Valerian was not another Jef who wept and wanted to

114

go home to his mother and father. He was a grown man, though no bigger than Jef had been, with a thin, peevish little voice because he had been woken up too soon and made to do something that he did not feel like doing.

The Horse Crone trundled the brown box over to the middle of the deck and began cranking the handle, at the same time beckoning Japetus to come on board. Silas never saw him actually come on board, for once again he was transported by loud music, for the second time in one day. He stared, dumbfounded. Was it a church she had there, a tiny little church?

Behind him Japetus scrambled on board. He had made up his mind that an old Gypsy woman with a barrel organ was nothing to be really frightened of, or a dwarf or a dancing bear. They were all things he had seen before in the big autumn markets. He went over and stood beside Silas.

The Horse Crone turned and turned the crank handle and the bear rose up on its hind legs and swayed and turned round and round. Silas felt almost as if he were flying through the air from bliss and he looked far out over all the flat cargo vessels along the quay.

A head appeared in one place. Someone who wanted to find out what was happening. All around several more heads popped up, but no one ventured all the way out. Everyone kept his eyes on what was happening without showing himself.

Valerian just stood there shaking himself. Most of all he wanted to creep back down the ladder and sleep some more; he was not used to being woken up at this time.

"You stay right here, sweetie," ordered the Horse Crone, who saw exactly how he was edging back toward the ladder. "You know perfectly well you're not finished yet."

"With what?" asked Valerian, sounding as if he did not understand what she meant.

"I do my part and you do yours, right?" said the Horse Crone, holding him fast with her nasty eyes.

Valerian shrugged; he thought that they usually didn't put on performances until evening.

"Not true," repeated the Horse Crone with a voice that nearly swept the little man down into the hole.

Obediently he began to do his stunts but he was not enjoying it. And Silas was not impressed; he could do just as good ones himself. What interested him was how the woman managed to wring music out of a polished wooden box. For she herself was definitely not playing the way he did on his flute; she was just turning a bar with a crank handle.

"Could I try?" he asked suddenly.

The Horse Crone's long yellow teeth appeared in what was meant to be an obliging smile, and Silas noticed that some more were missing, more than before. Without any objection, she handed it over to him, the box and handle and all, and then planted herself over by the gunwale where she would have the best view, both of her own ship and her neighbors'.

Surprised, Silas started turning the shiny smooth handle as the Horse Crone had done, until he found the right speed, the one that made the music sound the way it should, and he turned and turned with all his attention focused on the sounds that whelmed up, without noticing that Valerian stopped his acrobatic capers and was now standing next to the woman in the black skirts. The two murmured together and Japetus came over and tugged at Silas' arm saying that they should leave now. But it was out of the question for Silas to tear himself away from the miracle taking place between his hands, this tiny church that thundered when he touched it.

All of a sudden Japetus stiffened.

Out from one of the other barges crept two men, in the direction of the tree where the horses were tethered.

Japetus pulled Silas' arm so hard this time that first a completely wrong chord was sounded and then nothing at all.

"The horses!" he shouted in the unexpected silence.

Silas turned his head with a start and saw exactly what Japetus had seen, and like a shot he was already on his way across the deck toward the gunwale. Now they would have to be swift if they wanted to prevent the strangers from taking the two animals, each of which was valuable and which together represented a small fortune.

The Horse Crone stood by the gunwale following what was happening very carefully indeed. Silas headed for the gunwale right beside her and jumped, but to his great surprise he felt himself grabbed by her iron hands in the midst of his leap and he was hauled back into her domain. In a second she had twisted both his arms behind his back and there she held him while Valerian trussed up Japetus' legs, casting his own short, stocky body upon the boy.

"Now tell me, do you think we work for nothing just to entertain you?" snarled the Horse Crone when she could make herself heard once more.

"But they're stealing our horses!" spluttered Silas, wincing and groaning when she tugged his arms to emphasize her words.

"You can damn well pay for the performance before you run off. This way it looks far too much as if you planned to cheat me."

"But they're stealing our horses," Silas tried again.

"So much the better," snapped the Horse Crone. "Then the payment will come a little faster. . . . Well, out with the money," she went on when neither boy said anything.

"I have no money," muttered Silas, annoyed. "If you think we wander around with a fortune in our pockets, you're mistaken."

"What about him? Hasn't he anything either?"

Japetus lay with his face pressed down against the deck not answering.

Then she ordered, "Search him!"

And Valerian searched through his prisoner's pockets without finding anything except small coins. The Horse Crone was blatantly disappointed.

"You come here and order us to appear and put on a performance," she yelled, "and then you don't have what God has put in your pockets."

"We didn't order anything," said Silas, able to turn his head just enough to see Japetus stretched out full length on the deck. The little man was sitting on top of him, holding him in such a way that Japetus could not move even though he was much the bigger of the two. Although the manikin reached no great height, he apparently had plenty of strength. Japetus surrendered beneath him. Only Silas could see the two men untie

118

the horses and lead them across the quay into an alley-way. He poured a stream of curses over the Horse Crone as to how she could let that happen but she merely grinned maliciously and suggested that one horse more or less would not make very much difference to Alexander Planke.

Silas avoided telling her that one horse was his own.

But in any event they had to wait there while she had a message conveyed to the merchant's house for as much money as such a performance evidently cost.

Japetus groaned when he heard that. And Silas understood that his father was not one to joke in any way if anyone had been disobedient.

"Let me go home myself and get the money," Japetus asked. "I have plenty of money myself. It's bad enough that the horses are gone, but if he discovers that I have been in a place like this, he will be furious."

"Is that so?" asked the Horse Crone with that malevolent mildness she had acquired since the last time Silas had spoken with her.

Japetus nodded as well as he could with his face mashed down on the deck.

"And you·did intend to try making music from our organ, too, didn't you?"

"Yes," said Japetus.

"And he has already laid out a lot of money to let you go to school so that you can learn to cheat poor people in the best conceivable way."

"No one in our house cheats," protested Japetus indignantly.

"But you do go to school?"

"All decent people do."

119

"And such a big man as Alexander Planke would not be especially delighted to find that his son and heir had drowned in the river, right?"

Japetus mumbled inaudibly. Silas began to suspect what she was leading up to.

"He would certainly pay a great deal to get you back in good shape, right?"

Japetus did not reply and the Horse Crone turned her attention to Silas.

"What about you?" she began. "What do you think your father will pay to be able to fish you out of the river?"

"Nothing," said Silas.

"Stop that nonsense. Who is your father?"

"I don't have one."

"Don't try to fool me. If you won't tell me yourself, I'll find out anyway. No one goes around looking like a rich man's son without a father. . . . Unless your mother is a rich widow," she added thoughtfully.

Silas did not reply.

"Well, is your mother a widow?" the Horse Crone shouted in his ear, pulling one of his arms.

"No, she is not a widow," hissed Silas.

"But rich, then? She's rich, isn't she?"

"No," groaned Silas, wishing that he could manage to bite the ugly old woman's shoulder.

"Liar," noted the Horse Crone, stretching one arm out for a coil of rope with which she bound Silas until he was flat on the deck unable to move a finger. Then she prodded him with her foot and grinned.

"You remind me of someone or other," she said.

"But not of anyone good," she added menacingly.

"And don't go thinking that you can get out of this more cheaply as a result."

Then she left. Silas could hear from the tramp of her boots that she went from the quay toward the houses. Shortly after, she returned with a scrap of paper and a big goose feather.

"Sit him up," she said to Valerian, who immediately got off Japetus.

"You said that you know how to write?"

"Yes."

"Then write," she commanded.

Japetus studied the feather carefully. "This won't do," he said. "It has to be sharpened."

The Horse Crone jabbed her mistrusting eyes into him.

"Sharpened?" she asked.

"You can't write with a feather unless it is sharpened," insisted Japetus, feeling his wrist to see whether anything was broken. "And you have to have ink," he added.

"Ink? Tell me, didn't you go to school?"

"Yes," said Japetus, "but obviously you didn't. No one can write with a feather that was just ripped out of a goose's wing."

"Then sharpen it yourself," said the Horse Crone.

Japetus stuck his hand in his pocket and found his penknife, sharpened the feather to a point slowly and carefully, split the tip, and tested it on the back of his hand.

"There," he said. "And what did you think I would dip it in?"

The Horse Crone glared at him angrily and Silas was

impressed by how calmly Japetus took the situation. An entirely different Japetus had appeared, and Silas had the feeling that this other one had something up his sleeve.

"I didn't tell you to dip it," crowed the Horse Crone. "I told you to write."

Japetus scratched across the scrap of paper and showed it to the woman beside him.

"I need some ink," he said.

"Blood," came the grim word from Valerian.

"Shut up!" shouted the Horse Crone. "We're not going to have any nonsense with the town constable."

"Chicken blood, of course," said the dwarf, with a straight face.

The Horse Crone scowled at him.

"They must have something of that nature over in the tavern," continued the little man.

She went away again and returned shortly with some black liquid in a cup.

"Where's the rest of the bird?" asked Valerian. "Didn't you get that too?"

She did not reply but thrust the cup right under his nose and the little man was nauseated by the sight of it. Afterwards she held it right in front of Japetus, who was sitting on the deck trying not to do anything rash. He had no desire to have the dwarf on top of him again.

"What is it?" he asked.

"Ale," replied the Horse Crone at once triumphant and furious. "Ale with chimney soot in it. Now write."

"Well," said Japetus, dipping the quill pen. "What shall I write?"

"That your father has to pay to get you back, of

course." The words came impatiently from the Horse Crone.

Japetus laid the scrap of paper on the deck and wrote. The whole of one side was covered and the Horse Crone's small black eyes darted from the pen and the black, blotched letters to the back of Japetus' bent neck.

"What are you writing?" she wanted to know.

"That my father has to pay so he can get me back, of course," said Japetus.

"Read it." Her voice was extremely mistrustful.

Japetus looked up swiftly. Then he took the paper and intoned in a reading-aloud voice:

"To Merchant Alexander Planke. Honorable Father—"

The Horse Crone interrupted with a satisfied grunt, and Japetus continued to read aloud from the formal letter how he beseeched and implored his father to pay the ordered amount immediately so that they might be swiftly released from their imprisonment.

"How much shall I put down?" asked the merchant's son, turning over the page.

"What do you mean?"

"How much money do you want in exchange for setting us free?"

The Horse Crone stroked her long chin with a contented smile and named an enormous sum. Silas gave a start but Japetus went right on writing expressionlessly, and within seconds the other side of the page was covered with words as well.

With a side glance at Silas, Japetus handed it to the Horse Crone, who studied it thoroughly as if she were reading over what was written.

"You should put it in an envelope," admonished Japetus.

"Why is that?" The Horse Crone was always on her guard.

"Well," said Japetus, explaining, "if someone happened to read that in a short while you would be walking around with that much money under your skirts, you'd just get killed on your way and then we'd never be freed."

"You're not so bad after all." She grinned with pleasure and ordered Valerian to tie Japetus up the same way that Silas was tied and to make sure that neither of them got free.

After that she went over to the tavern on the other side of the quay for the third time. And now she stayed away for a long time.

"Where did she go?" asked Silas, turning his face more or less toward Valerian, who was sitting on the deck beside the two bound and captive boys. The dwarf's face was old and melancholy and looked all wrong with his tiny body.

"She's probably looking for a suitable messenger," was Valerian's opinion.

"Who does she consider suitable?" Silas wanted to know.

"Someone she can rely on. Someone she can completely trust with money."

"Do you really think someone will come back and deliver such an enormous sum of his own free will?" Silas stated scornfully. "The fellow who is dumb enough to do that does not deserve any better."

124

"It's not going to be just a fellow," said Valerian, "in any case not a fellow such as you mean."

"Who then?"

"A mother, for example, who must hand over her little child as security. That would be considered suitable."

Valerian spoke calmly, almost disinterestedly, and Silas realized that there were some sort of rules for the delivery of ransom money; obviously not just anyone could be sent.

"What if the merchant won't pay that much?" Silas asked again. The sum that had been named seemed to him immense and impossible to pay.

"Then we would definitely be obliged to lose one of you overboard," Valerian supposed mildly. "And it would be you, most probably, since he is the son. It would certainly help make them more willing after they find you."

Silas shuddered at the thought of being eased overboard, all bound and tied. That brown, fast-flowing water on the other side of the barge would close over him and he would have no chance of getting free. He only wondered how Japetus, who had been so anxious about taking a horse from his father's stable and about riding into this poor neighborhood, could take all this so calmly.

EIGHT

The escape

WHEN THE HORSE Crone came back on board, one could both see and feel that she had somehow succeeded. Not that she said as much in words, but she radiated such cheerful confidence that she would triumph. On her way across the deck to the hatch, she scooped up Japetus and carried him down with her. Moments later she came back up and fetched Silas, and he had to marvel over the strength that was in that bony piece of woman, for it did not tax her in the slightest to have him hanging over her shoulders like a dead pig while she balanced her soldier boots down the ladder rungs.

In the bottom of the barge it was both roomier and more rotten than Silas had imagined, and he could not help thinking of her winter house, the old stable where she had lived when she still had Jef with her. Here, too, a massive heap of straw had been spread out and here, too, a cooking pot and other spare items were strewn about messily. Not far from the hatch a little fireplace had been built of stones.

The Horse Crone carried Silas into the darkness and dumped him down in the straw next to Japetus.

"Now they can just stay here," she said.

"How long?" Silas wanted to know.

"Until I have the money here in my hand." She grinned triumphantly, stretching her arm up into the air with widespread fingers.

Then she found a piece of bread and went up on deck and divided it between Valerian and the bear. Shortly after, the boys heard Valerian being ordered to carry the music box ashore. Then there was silence.

"They're leaving!" exclaimed Silas in astonishment.

"They're probably going off to perform," murmured Japetus.

"Meanwhile we have to lie here like a couple of corn sheafs strung up for Christmas." Silas' voice was resentful at the prospect of possibly having to spend several hours like this.

"Do you think your father will pay?" he asked in a low voice.

"No," declared Japetus.

Silas sighed at the prospect of being thrown into the river.

"I think he'll join forces with the town guards right away," chuckled Japetus.

"The town guards?" repeated Silas incredulously.

"I wrote him where we were and who had captured us and what the place looks like," said Japetus.

Silas turned his head and tried to see him in the dark. "But—" he said.

Japetus laughed.

"I thought you said something quite different," Silas said quietly.

"That was just what I pretended to read."

And again Silas had to realize how useful it was to be able to read and write. How long would it take to learn? When Japetus wrote, it looked terribly easy and fast, but then he had been in school for a long time.

Silas began to feel faintly curious about what school was like. But of course he would have to stay in one place; it would not work if he moved somewhere else right in the middle of it all. He thought back to his good, impulsive wandering life and tried to imagine living differently. The only one who had ever seriously tried to teach him anything was Philip the sword-swallower— but he had run away from Philip before much came of that instruction.

Silas thought about how he actually could have become a skilled sword-swallower by now. . . . Or he could have become the boy who mucked out the stable for Bartolin the horse trader if he had not taken matters into his own hands. Neither alternative appealed to him. That was why he wanted to know something more about what school was like.

For a very long time it was quiet in the barge where the two boys lay; the water lapped and gurgled gently against the outer side of the hull, and from the hatch, which was the only source of light, the evening sun slanted down into the room. It was late in the day. Somewhere or other some children were playing.

Suddenly Silas noticed that he had been asleep. He woke at the sound of someone walking up on the deck and looked over toward the hatch from which no more sunlight was coming, only gray twilight. No one came down the stairs, not the Horse Crone, not Valerian or the bear. Nevertheless, he concluded that they must have returned, for someone was walking heavily up there with iron determination, surely the Crone with her soldier's boots.

Japetus also lay there listening.

"What do you think they're doing?" he whispered.

"It sounds like more than two people," Silas whispered back.

"Do you think it is someone looking for us?"

"I don't know," whispered Silas. "You mean the constable?"

"Yes. Should we shout?"

"I don't think it sounds like the guard," said Silas hesitantly.

"But listen! Now horses are coming!" exclaimed Japetus.

They both listened and definitely heard the clatter of hoofs up on the cobbles.

"They did come!" Japetus said breathlessly. "Listen— let's both shout at the same time."

"Hush," whispered Silas. Then he said, "It's work-horses. Listen for yourself."

And all too clearly Japetus heard the heavy slow

tread along the quay. But still he thought, "They're coming closer."

Right next to the Horse Crone's barge they came to a halt and the boys could hear the former knife-grinder give an order as to how they should be hitched up and something about poles. There was a burst of activity on deck, and various men's voices mingled with the Horse Crone's commands.

"They're moving the barge!" exclaimed Japetus in horror. "They're hauling it somewhere else."

"How do you know?"

"I can hear it. They always move them this way."

And sure enough, the barge began to move, the horses got slowly under way, and a couple of men shouted curt warnings to each other.

"They keep it clear of the quay and the other barges by using long poles," explained Japetus.

Silas noticed that the water was slapping against the wood in a new way. The barge was sailing. The whole big wretched hull was gliding forward through the water, drawn by a team of workhorses on land.

"Where do you think she means to move the barge?" Silas asked.

"I don't know."

"Far away?"

"There's no way of knowing."

"Underhanded old witch," murmured Silas. "They won't be able to find us."

"It's a safety precaution," Japetus supposed. "It needn't be very far."

Suddenly they could feel the barge swing around and head in another direction.

"Does the river fork?" Silas asked in a whisper.

"No, it must be one of the canals leading into the city."

"Do you know the place?"

"No," said Japetus. "I've only heard about it."

Silas marveled. Imagine living in a town and not knowing how it was laid out. As for himself, he didn't have to be in a new place very long before he had explored it all and knew a little about where things were. He thought you should always have a look at what there is to see. But Japetus apparently knew only those parts of town where people of his own sort lived and where he could go about without calling attention to himself.

"Do you think she would seriously consider throwing us into the water?" Japetus asked anxiously.

"Yes, if she could profit by it," replied Silas with conviction.

"But then she wouldn't get the money," Japetus pointed out.

"Well, she might want to remove the proofs that she had tried to get ransom money. . . . I mean, say she finds out that the constable suspects her and is looking for her. Once we are floating in the water, anyone could have thrown us in."

Japetus sighed sadly.

"Come on, we're not dead yet," said Silas comfortingly.

The heavy horses plodded sedately along with the barge which occasionally scraped against what, from the sound of it, could have been other barges. Then it was shaken through and through by a mighty bump and came to a stop. Up on deck feet ran in all directions and orders were given and received in lowered voices. Even the Horse Crone cut her knife-grinding voice by half. Apparently, thought Silas, the point is not to attract too much attention.

The boys lay silently listening for a while; there was no telling what might happen now, but Silas guessed that would be all for the night. Such things took time, and it would not pay for the woman to part with them prematurely unless she felt threatened. They heard the horses walk away, and with them presumably the helpers she had had for the move; in any case everything became very quiet. Only her own heavy boots took a couple of turns crisscrossing the deck as if something had to be attended to or put in place. Then she too went ashore and Valerian came creeping down the ladder and fumbled around in the dark.

They could hear him cursing quietly and hunting carefully around the little hearth. It sounded as if he were laying a fire and then sure enough he lit one. With a burning piece of wood raised over his head like a smoking torch, he came over and looked at Silas and Japetus lying like a couple of long bundles side by side, unable to move very much more than their eyes.

The dwarf appeared satisfied by the sight of their immobility.

"I'm thirsty," said Silas.

Without a word the little man got a clay jug of water, brought it over, and let Silas drink while he supported the back of his head.

"Would you like some too?" Valerian asked, offering the jug to Japetus.

Japetus nodded.

"Why did she move the barge?" Silas asked when the man had put the jug back.

"For safety's sake," said Valerian, sitting down in the straw beside them.

"Where are we now?"

"You'll find that out soon enough," asserted the dwarf.

"Where has she gone this time?"

"You ask too many questions, my boy. Just take it easy, then everything will work out, you'll see. Provided the money is delivered—"

"What if it isn't?"

"It will all work out, do you hear."

"This is a damn fine way for things to work out," fumed Silas.

Shivering, Valerian laid a couple of pieces of firewood on the fire. "It's chilly up there," he commented.

To change the subject, thought Silas. And perhaps also because he was afraid of the Horse Crone.

"Did she take the bear with her?" Japetus wanted to know.

"No, it's her watchdog," explained Valerian.

"What kind of watchdog? Can it bark?"

"It's up on deck in case anyone happens to think of climbing on board."

Valerian rubbed his chilly hands together, evidently glad that he was not the one who had to walk around up there for the rest of the night.

Just then all three of them froze and listened. The sound of a shout and distant disturbance forced its way down through the open hatch and Valerian's face took on an anxious expression.

"What is it?" Silas asked innocently. "Is there a celebration somewhere?"

Valerian shook his head and went on listening. The two boys exchanged telling looks. They felt sure that they knew what it was.

"I'm the one who has to toss you into the water if they come here," said the little man sadly.

Both boys stared at him: Did he know that too?

"It sounds as though they have found the old place—but then it was an excellent description," he added.

"What description?" asked Japetus, trying to conceal how shaken he was.

"Oh, stop it!" laughed the dwarf. "You wrote it."

"You can read!" Silas and Japetus almost shouted both together.

"Yes," said Valerian quietly.

"But—but—what now?" Neither of them had reckoned with this possibility.

"Does she know?" Silas asked cautiously.

Valerian shook his head.

"You haven't told her?"

"No."

There was a short silence.

"Why not?" asked Japetus in astonishment. "After all, you work for her."

"Why should I? She was the one who thought of taking you prisoners and demanding ransom. Besides, she doesn't know what I can—and what I can't—do—except for somersaults and that kind of thing. That's why I'm still the one who will toss you overboard if trouble comes too close," he added grimly.

135

"How do you happen to be able to read?" asked Silas when he had collected himself a little.

"Once I belonged to a rich nobleman," said Valerian, "and I didn't waste time while I was in his house."

Silas immediately promised himself that if he managed to get away from there he too wanted to learn to read and write. If Valerian could, then he could too, after all.

"I had better go up and keep an eye on the way the battle is going," said the dwarf, starting to clatter up the ladder.

"Why can't you just set us free?" Silas called after him. "You could say that you *had* tossed us into the water."

Valerian turned around.

"Soon I will be an old man," he said solemnly. "I have to earn the necessities of life in one way or another and she is the only person who will have me."

Then he vanished.

No sooner had his short, bent legs disappeared up into the darkness than Silas started to wiggle around.

"What is it?" whispered Japetus.

"Double up your legs and give me a push," Silas whispered back, twisting the rope as much as he could.

"What are you going to do?"

"Over by the fire."

Japetus bent his legs as far as he could and shoved Silas in the direction of the fire. Outside in the pale darkness the commotion increased. It was undoubtedly the town guards storming around where the barge had been moored before it was moved. It sounded as if there were many men.

Japetus shoved Silas again carefully and as soon as Silas was close enough he put his feet up over the masonry edge and in above the flames.

Soon after, a new smell spread out into the room.

"You're on fire!" Japetus warned him fearfully. "The flames are burning you. Doesn't it hurt?"

"That's mostly my shoes, but I have to do it," groaned Silas.

Directly over the fire the rope fibers curled up like little black hairs and the rope undid itself in flames. Silas whipped his legs out onto the floor and kicked himself free.

"It's a great trick to have been rolled up this way," he mumbled as he wiggled out.

"Trick!" exclaimed Japetus. "I think it's loathsome. Something has bitten me on the back and I can't even scratch myself."

"Oh well," said Silas, "it's probably just a flea and that's not dangerous. It would have been worse if they'd bound us hand and foot." He undid the last bit and set to work on Japetus and seconds later they were both free.

Japetus sat up and wiggled his shoulders and cracked his knuckles to get his body working again, then he scratched himself energetically under his clothes.

"There is nothing like scratching oneself," he said.

"No," said Silas, standing up. "It's like getting food when you're famished."

Cautiously they began creeping toward the ladder in the faint glow from the low fire.

"What if he's sitting up there waiting for us?" whispered Japetus.

"We're two against one," asserted Silas, "and he's not that big."

"No, but he's strong," whispered Japetus, not wanting to renew his acquaintance with Valerian's small, plump, iron fists. "He had a hard grip," he said.

Silas scrambled soundlessly up the ladder and stuck his head out to spy into the night air that smelt of wet refuse and crumbling wood. There was silence on the barge and silence on land, but it was just the opposite of silent over where they had been moored before. Neither Valerian nor the bear were to be seen and Silas hoped inwardly that the former had gone ashore and that the latter had fallen asleep.

He stuck his hand down in the hatch and signaled for Japetus to follow him, and single file they crept up onto the deck. There they paused to listen, trying to form an impression of their surroundings, which was not easy in the darkness. But there were houses in any case; there were many lighted windows and they could see the edges of roofs against the green-black sky. They were still within the city limits, and really the only thing to do was to jump ashore and disappear.

But it was not going to be that easy. The moment they started across the deck, they were greeted by a throaty sound in front of them and the faint scraping of claws on the planks. Japetus started and grabbed Silas' jacket in terror.

"Stand still," murmured Silas in a low voice, while he rooted about in the clothes that he still did not feel comfortable wearing. "It won't do anything if you stand still."

Silas could feel the warm breath from the open jaws

right in front of him. So this was what Valerian meant about the bear being a watchdog. Now it was easier to understand how Valerian could leave the deck. With some difficulty Silas extracted the flute and started playing softly and soothingly.

The bear closed its mouth and shook its head and the boys could hear its chain rattle. So it was chained—though with such a long lead that it could cover most of the ship. No one could climb on board—or leave the ship—unassailed.

But the music had greater power over the animal than its training as a watchdog: submissively it rose up onto its hind legs and started circling round and round as they had seen it do earlier in the afternoon. Very slowly the boys backed away toward the gunwale, but just as they were about to climb off Silas bumped into someone standing there.

"Watch where you're going!" bellowed Valerian's voice in the dark.

Silas and Japetus jumped to one side and turned to face him, convinced that he intended to throw himself upon them and prevent their escape. But nothing happened.

"What are you waiting for? Aren't you going to go?"

Valerian hoisted his compressed man's body up on the gunwale and sat there in the dark like a big cat.

Silas and Japetus stood tense and motionless. Behind them the bear toppled down on all fours and came over and sniffed for his reward.

"Why do you say that?" asked Silas, making no attempt to get past the dwarf.

"I just thought it looked as if you were about to

scram," pronounced Valerian in a more conciliatory tone.

There was a brief silence.

Then, as they still neither moved nor spoke, he continued, "You can just go."

"Why?" asked Silas again.

"Then I get out of having to drown you. It's not my fault that you got away: I didn't free you. . . . Remember that, should I happen to seek employment with Alexander Planke some day," he added with what appeared to be a wry smile.

"She'll be furious when she finds out," said Silas.

"Exactly," said Valerian. "I don't concern myself with wrathful furies."

"But you did help tie us up," recalled Japetus.

"I have to do what I'm told—until I find a new master. Do I have any prospect of that now?"

The question was quite definitely directed to Japetus, but it was Silas who answered with a new question.

"Have you performed in a circus?"

"That was many years ago," said Valerian sadly.

"Do you know anything about horses?"

"I'm too old to work on horseback now. Not sure enough, you understand. I've also been away from it too long."

"I don't mean perform—can you look after them?"

"Oh yes, of course I can look after them."

"I never thought of that," said Japetus apologetically.

"I can't promise you," Silas went on speaking to Valerian, "but Alexander Planke does need a stableboy."

"You certainly think of everything," Japetus interrupted again, half marveling and half annoyed that he had not thought of it himself. "I'll tell Father about you," he said to Valerian. "Can we go now?"

"That you must decide for yourselves. I have neither seen nor heard anything," promised the voice. "And remember, I can do many more things than just look after horses."

"But you could have freed us a long time ago," said Silas.

"No," said Valerian. "What if she kicked me out before I had another place to go to? You both should realize that I have to be careful because of my appearance. People find fault with me terribly easily, assuming that I am not a real person. They prefer to think of me as some kind of animal."

"Then why didn't you stay with the nobleman?" asked Japetus.

"Oh, that is a long story. And if I were you I wouldn't waste time on it now."

The boys approached hesitantly, the dwarf never budged, but they didn't dare believe him until they were standing on solid ground again.

They still had a long way to go, and it was not easy to hurry in an unfamiliar neighborhood when they couldn't even see where to put their feet. Most of the lights were already out in spite of the steadily approaching uproar—or perhaps precisely because of it. To be sure, no one wanted to draw the constabulary's attention to his house. Therefore Silas and Japetus each quite literally stretched out one hand and felt his way forward along the walls of the houses, and they also had to pay attention where to step. The gutter stones in the middle of the street were full of thrown-out excrement and filth and since the street was extremely narrow, there was not much space to maneuver in. Besides, it stank. Silas found all this less than pleasing, and more than once they stumbled over bodies that felt like dead animals, but they didn't take the time to find out whether that was what they were.

If it was nasty for Silas, it was much, much worse for Japetus, accustomed as he was to the more refined side of city life. It was overwhelming for him to have to walk through this foul-smelling level of life, where only poverty was plentiful, and where he knew that people of his sort could all too easily be struck down and robbed of everything.

But at the same time it was clear to him that they had no choice. The danger of remaining on the river barge and waiting for the constable to find his way to them was too great. A woman like the Horse Crone would not hesitate to make sure that they disappeared in the river if by that she could save her own skin. They had to find a way through this confusion of small winding alleys as fast as possible, where small, low huts, the roofs of which they could touch without difficulty, alternated with tall, narrow houses that rose up into the air, virtually leaning out over the alley where they were walking. All they had to go by was the noise from the quay, where the guards seemed to have undertaken a larger search of all the houses, under vehement protest from the inhabitants. Silas was sure that no one would be searched willingly, neither a family nor an individual. Every single one had something they did not want to have brought to light, whether it was stolen goods, liquor stills, or other infamies. This made for solidarity, Silas thought as he fumbled on; in a way this was a good place.

Nevertheless his spirits lightened as they gradually approached the quay where they had been that afternoon.

"At least they have some light there," he said over his shoulder to Japetus.

"The guards' torches," the other boy explained.

"Yes," said Silas, tripping over a stoop that protruded into the street.

"Up you get, sonny," said a voice from the darkness next to the wall. Both Silas and Japetus stepped back into the middle of the street.

"He's drunk," mumbled Japetus.

"He is not in the least drunk," said the voice. "He is quite the opposite."

A long arm came out of the dark and grabbed Japetus by the scruff of his neck.

"What are you doing here?"

"Nothing." Japetus winced.

"Is that so?" said the voice sarcastically. "You take the time to wander around in the middle of the night instead of sleeping, do you? You want me to believe that?"

"Are you from the town guard?" asked Silas, coming closer.

The man in the darkness laughed contemptuously. "They're dashing around howling like a pack of wild animals—they won't find anything that way."

"What are they looking for?" asked Silas cautiously.

"The same thing I am," said the voice. "But I'm having a good deal more success."

"What do you mean?"

"Well, as far as I can tell, I've caught a fellow who,

143

to judge from his clothing, does not belong to this here part of town."

"All the same we do live right down the alley here," said Silas calmly. "We were just going to see what all that noise is."

"Really?" said the voice, convinced that this was not true.

"Let's have a look over here in the light."

To the boys' astonishment, the stranger did not try to rob them of everything or drag them into a darker side alley as Silas had feared. Instead, they all groped their way forward in the direction of the flickering lights. But he did not let go of Japetus.

Seconds later they were standing amidst a crowd of angry people who felt wronged by the town guards' accusations.

"There, you can see for yourselves!" yelled a coarse woman's voice. "We weren't the one who hid them." She pointed at the boys with an accusing index finger. "It wasn't us at all. They ran away themselves and we have nothing to do with that woman bear trainer."

Silas blinked at this violent broadside and caught sight of a couple of men from the guard who were pushing their way forward. He turned to Japetus and saw that it was the handyman Carnelian who was holding him by the scruff of the neck while he gesticulated and exclaimed to the best of his ability. A guard seized Silas. They also wanted to take Japetus away but Carnelian protested that he intended to deliver him personally. All of them looked as if they feared that the boy would disappear between their very fingers. They held onto them as if they were dangerous criminals.

"I can walk perfectly well by myself," said Japetus.

"You stay right where you are," said the handyman. "I was the one who found you and I intend to hold onto you."

"Where is Father?"

"He's coming; someone went to fetch him. He has a coach here somewhere. . . . I'm the one who will get the money."

"What money?" Japetus wanted to know.

"Your father offered a reward to the person who could bring you back alive."

"Only for me?" asked Japetus surprised. "Why not for Silas?"

"Most likely he can look forward to something quite different."

Silas looked sharply at Carnelian; the anxiety their disappearance had caused could still be discerned in the handyman. The guards had not retreated but stood holding the huge crowd of people in control with their eyes. It was not especially pleasant, he thought, to stand accountable in the middle of such a crowd.

Just then Alexander Planke's closed coach drove up and the boys were ordered in without anyone asking where they had been or what had happened to them. But Silas could see from Japetus that they would not get off that lightly.

NINE

Trial and judgment

DURING THE ENTIRE journey home through the night-quieted town, no one spoke. Alexander Planke's face was closed and somber and on the seat facing him the two boys sat silently waiting for the merchant's anger to burst out of him. But nothing happened. Silas found it an unbelievable strain to sit there prepared to refute the man's possible complaints, yet not given a chance to say anything. He would much rather have had it over with immediately, even if that meant that he himself would be shown the door.

He glanced at Japetus surreptitiously and could suddenly see how closely he resembled his father, the same brooding somberness that did not find release in words—perhaps slightly more oppressed in the son and somewhat more preoccupied in the father—but still the same expression of a state of mind.

Up in the kitchen the boys were ordered to eat and wash and go to bed. It was late and Alexander Planke did not want to talk with them until the next morning, he said, disappearing into the front rooms.

Japetus sighed.

"Of course I will tell your father that it was all my fault," Silas comforted Japetus, digging valiantly into the warmed-up leftovers of dinner which Anna set before them with displeasure. What did they mean by this? she asked: making her get out of her good, warm bed to wait on such a pair of pups. As if it weren't enough that they had gone and panicked the whole house, now she also had to spend her good sleep time setting out food for them. She walked back and forth dressed in her shift and night bonnet, grumbling to herself, but neither Silas nor Japetus was overly concerned by her protests. Different serious matters tormented them.

"It's no use," asserted Japetus. "Only one thing counts here in this house, and that is what Father says. And when he says that I'm not allowed to take a horse without asking, he means it. So it does no good for you to insist that it was your fault."

"Well," said Silas, "if he kicks you out too, I'll definitely take you with me."

He didn't sound particularly depressed by the thought, but Japetus raised his head with a start.

"Dad wouldn't kick anyone out; that's not the way he is. Not you either. Once he has said that you can live

148

here and learn something, he means it. What he says always goes."

"Not with me," said Silas.

Japetus looked at him searchingly.

"I am not sure I want to stay here," said Silas and then he finished chewing.

"But Dad has said that you're welcome to stay."

"He can't start ordering me around like that, simply because I happened to catch his horses."

Silas could see that Japetus did not really understand what he meant. In this house people were all too used to obeying the master. The fact that someone might simply renounce the security that came from being under this protective wing, just for the right to decide things for himself, was something that Japetus could not comprehend.

"It's a real shame about the dapple," muttered Silas absently.

Japetus was silent; he badly needed to get to bed after the eventful day. A horse was a horse, and since it was gone, there was nothing to be done about it.

"But most probably it could be got back one way or other," continued Silas.

Japetus shook his head sadly.

"Impossible."

"Why not? They must be somewhere, both of them. It doesn't pay to slaughter animals like that."

"Not in this town. You saw for yourself what happened. How do you think anyone could find a couple of horses in that kind of neighborhood?"

Silas did not answer, but he was not at all sure that

Japetus was right. He shoved his plate away, said good night and went up to his room, where clean clothes had been laid out again on the bed.

"God, what a waste!" thought Silas, looking down at himself. Needless to say, what he had put on that morning was not too terribly clean anymore, but to change right away was almost too much.

On the other hand, his own clothes had disappeared. Silas looked around in the corners of the little room; there didn't seem to be very many places where they could have got mislaid, and he felt sure that they had been on the chair. He looked under the quilt. Anna or Thea or whoever had tidied the bed might have hidden them there. But he found nothing underneath nor on the floor under the bed, not even his leather shoes.

Infuriated, he galloped back down to the kitchen where Anna had set about cleaning up after the late meal.

He asked her where the sheepskin coat was—and everything else.

"Thrown out," was all she said.

It did not escape him that her expression was one of disgust.

"Thrown out?" asked Silas as if he did not understand what she said.

"Exactly. The mistress told Thea to throw them out."

"Where?"

"On the rubbish heap, I daresay. Where else?"

"But," protested Silas, disconcerted, "those are my clothes."

He still thought of Japetus' clothes as a loan, which apparently the rest of the family did not.

150

So then he asked why.

"We can't have anything like that lying around," said Anna, putting the last utensils away. "The mistress said that you would have no further use for them."

Silas stood staring at her while thoughts rushed around inside his head.

Then he said, "Oh," and turned and went upstairs without making any attempt to walk quietly. But no sooner was he up in the room again than he whipped off the stiff and partially ruined shoes and stole back down in his bare feet past the kitchen door, on past the door to the shop and out into the yard. However, the rubbish pile was a large area and it was impossible to see what was what, now in the middle of the night. He had to get a candle.

His thoughts wandered to the lit candle beside his bed, but it would not be prudent to run all the way up there again—where else could he find a candle? From Carnelian? Silas thought that he was getting to know the handyman well enough so that he could walk in there and borrow his candle without endangering his life, and so, for a second time, he slipped into the broad, low room which smelled of so many things.

He walked over to the counter and called Carnelian in a whisper, but it was not Carnelian who darted out of the sleeping place and seized him. It was Tobias. They were both equally astonished.

"What are you doing here?" asked Silas.

"Sleeping, of course," came the proud reply from the stableboy who had obviously already changed his job. "I'm watching for burglars. . . . What do you want?"

"To borrow a candle," explained Silas truthfully.

"What for?" asked Tobias. Silas could clearly hear the fellow's mistrust. He had to explain himself in addition to justifying why he was creeping around the shop at night. So he hurriedly told him that Thea had thrown out his clothes and that he couldn't find them in the dark without stepping into all the muck.

Tobias lit the candle and went along with him out into the yard; he was new at his job and took his position seriously, but Silas quickly found what he was looking for. Fortunately it was all rolled up in a bundle and consequently not too filthy.

Then Silas said, "Has Carnelian moved over into the stable?"

"Only until another stableboy comes," said Tobias.

"One will soon," said Silas.

"How do you know?"

"I think so."

"The position hasn't been advertised yet."

"Something tells me that it's filled; I feel I can see it."

They went along back into the corridor and Tobias carefully replaced the iron bar while Silas started up the stairs with the bundle under his arm. But no sooner had Tobias crept off to his counter again and closed up after himself, than Silas turned back down and stole out into the yard and over to the stable, where he hid his clothes in a corner under a pile of straw.

Then he finally walked up to bed with the conviction that now at least not everything could go all wrong.

Early the following morning both boys were called in to Alexander Planke's office. Japetus was made very ill-at-ease by the situation; he had enormous respect for his father, while Silas was mostly distressed about the horses. If it hadn't been for the dapple . . . , he thought.

Alexander Planke demanded an explanation of where they had been and what had happened, and in his role as father he addressed his son first and foremost. But Japetus answered hesitantly and inarticulately so that for the most part it was Silas who ended up doing the talking.

"Don't you know that you cannot take a horse from the stable by yourself?" asked the merchant.

"Yes . . . ," mumbled Japetus.

"But it was my fault," said Silas. "I was the one who told him to."

"And what could you have possibly wanted to do in that part of town?" continued the merchant.

Japetus was silent.

"That was also my fault," said Silas again. "I was the one who said that we should go that way."

"Why, since Japetus knew perfectly well that he is not allowed to?"

"Japetus is old enough to make up his own mind where he wants to ride," asserted Silas.

"Is that so?" said the merchant sarcastically, raising one eyebrow. "But he acted unwisely and returned home without a horse."

"Japetus would not have ridden that way if he had been able to decide himself," said Silas. "He is much too used to doing what people tell him—but I'll definitely find the dapple for you."

Alexander Planke's expression became thoughtful and he sat quietly for a long while, so long that Silas repeated that he definitely would get the dapple back for him.

"I don't believe you can do that," said the merchant skeptically. "This is a large town and there is awesome solidarity in the poorest sections. They all protect each other from outsiders. Respectable people do well to keep away from there. A good deal happens in those narrow alleys that no one ever gets to hear about."

But Silas did not let himself be deterred; he was not a respectable person and he had no intention of giving up before he began.

"What happened to the bear trainer?" he asked.

"Oh, she was taken away by the town constable."

"And the dwarf?"

"He too."

"They will let him go," said Silas.

"Why?" protested Alexander Planke. "Wasn't he her accomplice in the ransom attempt, and didn't he also take part in catching and tying you up? Naturally he will receive his punishment."

"He only did what he was ordered to do," said Silas gravely.

"No excuse."

"That's unjust. The Horse Crone is also the kind of person who wants to control other people, and the dwarf could only choose between starving to death or doing what she said. . . . Besides, he was the one who refrained from throwing us into the river, and it was he who simply let us go once we had gotten untied."

"The Horse Crone?" asked Japetus and Alexander Planke simultaneously.

"Was she the one you told us about?"

"Yes," said Silas.

"Why didn't you say so?"

"Why should I? She didn't recognize me in these clothes and she tried to kill me once before. . . . But Valerian will not be put in prison."

"What good will that do if, as you say, he is to die of starvation anyway?" said Alexander Planke doubtfully.

"He will seek the position of stableboy here as soon as he is freed," said Silas. "He would be suitable—but he would probably need a stool to stand on when he curries the horses."

"That is for me to decide!" exclaimed the merchant, caught off guard. "You are aware that decision-making is up to me—but why is it that I have no say in this matter? . . . And how do you know for sure that he would be suitable for the job?"

"He has performed in a circus; he had an act with horses, and anyone who does that knows something about them."

Silas spoke without faltering; he really knew what he was talking about.

"But if he were to stay here, he would be obliged to conform to the ways and customs of this house," said the merchant, "which you will also do if you wish to remain here. I alone make decisions and that will continue to be the case."

"Yes," said Silas solemnly, "and that is also why I do not want to be here."

"What don't you want?"

The merchant's face looked dismayed. How could anyone refuse such an invitation!

"Have you no desire to learn anything?"

"Yes," said Silas, "I would like to go to school, and I have already learned a lot about living in a house like

155

this in a town like this. But I am much too used to doing what I feel like doing—and too many rows would come of it. . . . So when I've got hold of the horses I think I'll probably be off again."

Japetus stirred anxiously, but his father did not let him express himself. Instead he said that was a splendid idea, for then their tutors could instruct him in the meantime.

"In any event you must not think that I have forgotten that you stopped my runaway four-in-hand," added the merchant.

Silas looked up.

"If I had not been used to making my own decisions, I would not have done that," he said calmly. "I knew that it was my own responsibility if I broke my neck or got trampled on and ended up crippled."

Alexander Planke let his gaze rest on him in silence for a good long time, and Silas felt that the man behind the big desk inwardly acknowledged that he was right. And he could see the doubt in the merchant's eyes when he shifted his gaze to his well-brought-up son.

Japetus could count and write and already knew a good deal about business, but whose fault was it that he could not capture runaway horses?

"But in the future," Alexander Planke added in a gruff and final tone, "in the future neither of you should ask to borrow a horse."

Neither Silas nor Japetus protested. From the merchant's point of view, taking away the right to ride after such an excursion must seem a reasonable punishment.

"Just go ahead and take them," he continued after an almost imperceptible pause.

Both boys started, but before they were able to collect themselves, they were ordered to leave; Alexander Planke had other, more pressing matters to attend to than sitting in judgment that morning.

TEN

Silas begins his double life

SILAS OFFERED NO resistance when the merchant's children drew him along with them to their schoolroom where the tutor, Fabian Fedder, was waiting. He was not particularly enthusiastic about starting with a new pupil, and a pupil of low birth who lacked manners as well. Fabian Fedder expected the worst, and his expectations were not disappointed, because from the very first Silas demanded an explanation for why he should do as he was told.

Why should he begin on the first page of his copybook and not on one of the others? Why should he begin right at the end of each line—did it really make any difference? Japetus looked down at the tabletop and said nothing, but Ina and Jorim stared openly at the strange boy, baffled by such ignorance. Of course you began on the first page because—well, because that was the way it was done. There was absolutely no question that it could be done any other way.

Fabian Fedder explained to Silas painstakingly that to be able to read and write a certain order was essential, and that first he had to learn the different letters before he could begin to use them at all.

Silas supposed that this did make good sense, but it proved to be more difficult to keep the tiny black thingumajigs in order than he had imagined. He would have preferred to learn everything at once, and the teacher shook his head at such great impatience.

But Silas figured that if a small child like Jorim could write, then so could he. And since he was entirely convinced of the usefulness of being able to write and understand written letters, he put all his energy into learning them as quickly as possible. When Fabian Fedder announced that the lesson was over, Silas felt as though he had only just got started and said that it was stupid to stop just then.

Ina and Jorim tittered with delight over everything that Silas dared say to their tutor, and at all the extraordinary things he thought up. Even though the strange boy was wearing some of Japetus' clothes and happened to look like other boys they knew, his behavior was still completely different from what they were used to. And while Japetus, who of course had many years of school behind him, worked at different exercises on his own, Fabian Fedder was supposed to attend to Silas while teaching the two smaller children at the same time. Ina had already been studying for three years, while Jorim had been taught for only one. Silas marveled that it could take so long to learn so little, and deep inside he felt sure that it could go faster. When Fabian Fedder got up to leave, Silas went over to him with his copybook and asked to have all the letters of the alphabet written down, not only the three that he had to learn for the next day, but every letter there was.

Fabian Fedder gave a resigned sigh and wrote one on each page, convinced that this request was an example of beginner's eagerness and that his pupil would soon have had enough. Silas himself offered no explanation but a very large part of the afternoon he remained sitting in the schoolroom working his way through the book and before the evening meal he went over to the storeroom and got himself a board. When he appeared lugging it Japetus stared at it quite baffled. It was quite short and rather wide and he didn't understand what Silas wanted to do with it.

"I usually wake up very early in the morning," said Silas, "so I might as well use the time to write as to lie staring up at the ceiling."

Japetus looked at him with the same resigned, half-smiling expression that the tutor had put on, but Silas didn't care. As soon as he had eaten his evening meal he took his board and writing things and went up to his room, causing some resentment on the part of the other children, who would have liked some entertainment from his company.

But up there under the eaves Silas suddenly felt a powerful urge to move about, to get outdoors after a whole long day inside the house, and since it was not far for him from thought to action, he slipped unseen down the back stairs and over to the stable, where he put on his old clothes and hid his new ones. No one noticed him leave, and Silas hurried in the direction of the river neighborhood where he had nearly lost his life the previous day. He might as well start looking for the horses right away, he thought, and dressed in his old clothes he would not attract nearly as much attention. No one would dream that he had come from one of the richest houses in town.

Silas felt happily at ease when he came out onto the quay where the river barge had first been moored, and where now a group of half-grown boys and girls stood discussing what had happened the day before.

They stopped talking when Silas appeared and all faces turned toward him mistrustfully.

Silas greeted them but received only one unintelligible grunt in reply. Nevertheless he went on undaunted to inquire what the commotion had been about.

"Why do you care? Are you asking for someone else?"

Silas ignored the hostility and asked instead with interest whether they had been allowed out that late, whether they'd been there and seen it.

"Of course," they said proudly, interrupting each other while continuing to observe the stranger with distrust.

"If only I could have," sighed Silas.

"You're not allowed to go out?"

This was the first overture from the group and Silas shook his head sadly.

"Only until ten o'clock, then she locks the door."

He thought of the door to the merchant's court and how he must be home before Carnelian was supposed to lock up.

"Who?" asked a big boy who towered above the whole gang.

"The old witch," said Silas.

"Your mother?"

"She's dead. . . . My aunt. I have to live with her now."

"It's easy to see that you've only just come here," said a girl with coarse, unruly hair and hostile eyes.

"How?" Silas asked innocently, looking down.

The others laughed in a know-it-all way.

"We can hear it even when you talk. You're a country boy."

Silas shrugged in resignation, not protesting, implying that he could do nothing about it.

"Were you the ones who made the row yesterday evening?" he asked instead.

"Us?" They laughed raucously. "Not on your life!"

"Why?"

"It was the town constables."

"What did the constables want here?"

Silas looked around the peaceful strip along the water.

"Someone swiped a couple of horses," one of them explained.

"Horses?" Silas asked as if he did not understand.

"Yes, some fellows came from the rich end of town, and they climbed right onto the bear trainer's boat. They sure got what they deserved."

"What was that?" asked Silas.

"Well, she tied them up and threw them into the

bottom of the boat and demanded money to set them free."

"I thought you said it was a couple of horses," said Silas.

"Well, of course someone ran off with them, but it was the rich man's two sons that the town guards came after and they turned all the barges upside down and inside out. What a scene!"

"Did they find them?"

"Of course not. Naturally she'd moved the barge somewhere else, but they got her anyway; she was stupid enough to poke her nose into other people's business."

"What about the boys?"

"They got away by themselves and were picked up by a coach. They were no small fry; they have plenty of horses—a couple more or less makes no difference to them."

"But still horses are valuable," Silas asserted.

"Oh come on, they're loaded with money."

"I thought that sort was so tight-fisted that they'd never let anyone get away with something like that."

"They're tight-fisted, all right, but they don't stand a chance of getting them back."

Two boys spoke up for the gang and they resembled each other so closely that Silas guessed they were twins. They were neither particularly big nor was either one especially strong, but they were always in agreement and could think fast. Silas set about becoming friends with them first. Another boy was actually much bigger, probably capable of knocking down a grown man, but for all that he looked a little dense and no one paid much attention to what he said. His name was Theodore and he was the one who towered over all the others.

"But after all they have the whole town guard to help them, don't they?" Silas ventured.

That made them laugh a lot.

"Do you think the town guard can do anything in our part of town?" asked one of the twins. "They hardly dare come in here."

Then Silas asked, "Did she have a bear? I thought you said she was a bear trainer or something."

"It's walking around the deck of her barge and is completely crazy," one of them answered.

"Why?"

"No one is giving it anything, neither food nor water."

"Why not?"

"Because no one around here has more than enough to feed themselves."

"I've never seen a bear," lied Silas.

"Then come along and have a look," said the girl with the unruly hair. "If you dare."

"Is it dangerous?" Silas wanted to know.

The girl humphed scornfully.

"In fact, no one can go right up to the barge," she said.

Silas agreed to go along, and the whole gang trotted off down the alleys in the direction of the canal where the barge was now moored. Silas paid very careful attention to everything he saw.

"If only I had been there yesterday," he said while they were walking.

"Why?"

"Well, horses like that—or maybe you belong to the families who pinched them?"

Silas looked around questioningly. The others shook their heads.

"For something like that you could earn a reward."

"How could you do that? A reward? You can't get a reward for something stolen."

"By giving it back, you could," said Silas.

"You're crazy. A rich merchant like that—he deserves to be robbed."

"Maybe you know the people who took them?" Silas looked right at one of the twins. "Maybe you get a little something for keeping quiet about it."

The boy who was called Moritz let out a guffaw.

"Or someone else?" Silas looked around the gang.

"It sure is obvious from listening to you that you don't know much about anything," said the girl cuttingly.

No one else said anything but they all clearly shared the girl's opinion.

"Yes, we get something," murmured the other twin, who was called Mikael. "We get a beating if we don't keep quiet."

"So you don't even try? Don't you even have an inkling how much you could get for that?"

"For what?"

"For going to that damn merchant or whatever he is and selling the information about where he can find his nags."

"Let him go get them himself!" shouted the twins enthusiastically in one breath.

Silas grinned.

"Did you think I meant for you to lead them home yourselves?"

When they reached the canal, Silas saw that they were right about the bear, who was still tied so that it could walk around the deck. It had not been given anything to eat or drink since the previous day.

"I thought it was tame," said Silas when they stopped next to the Horse Crone's barge. "She certainly can't take that one anywhere with her."

The bear scowled at them and growled and snarled deep in its throat.

"That's because it's starving," said the girl with the hair.

"No one has given it anything," said another girl who had not spoken before.

"That's sad," Silas observed.

"It serves her right," said tall Theodore. "It'll die before she ever gets out again."

"But that's really not its fault," asserted Silas. "I mean I pity the bear."

"You can't go near it," stated Moritz.

"And no one can afford to give it anything," said Mikael.

"Well now, water doesn't cost all that much," Silas declared.

"Maybe you dare go up to it?" asked the girl with the unruly hair, looking straight at Silas.

"I don't know," said Silas hesitantly. "I might try."

"Damn it, I'd like to see that," stated Theodore, starting to swing his arms with pleasure. Several of the others also perked up at that.

167

Silas purposefully pretended not really to know what he should do, but the others eyed a chance for entertainment and brought over a sloshing tub of water in no time; who knows where they got it. Silas took the handle and the whole gang watched expectantly while he slowly approached the barge. The bear paced back and forth snarling right inside the gunwale and appeared to be neither in good spirits nor expecting anything from them.

Silas set the water down on the ground and, with his back turned to the others, took out his flute and slowly blew on it. Behind him silence fell but it took awhile for the bear to react, then it stopped and looked as if it were confused about something. Silas took advantage of this pause to walk closer and move the water tub forward. The bear snapped at him furiously and Silas had to stop again and play a little more on the flute. Then suddenly it rose up on its hind legs as if it wanted to dance and Silas quickly set the water down on the deck and withdrew a short distance. Not only did the animal have neither food nor drink, he thought, but apparently many people had also come and stared at it and probably tormented it. Whatever the case, all the small stones and pebbles strewn about the deck had not been there the day before. He waited until the bear had finished drinking, then he got it to dance again and it stood up for a long time staring at him when he walked back to the others carrying the empty tub.

"It's really terrible that we have nothing for him," he said quietly. "It must be terrible to have to stand there starving to death."

"Well, maybe the baker has some old bread," said one

of the twins. And once the thought had been thought, it did not take too long to send a couple of the smaller fellows off to find out. Meanwhile the others were very quiet and Silas guessed that it was because of his flute. They all stood around feeling caught by surprise and he was aware of distrust working away inside them again.

"Where did you get that?" asked Mikael, who wanted to see it. But Silas would not let it out of his hands; instead, he put it to his lips again and played a couple of melodies which Anna sang in the kitchen and which he thought they were sure to know.

Then he said, "It's old; I've had it for years." He didn't want the other boys to borrow it, and when the two who had been sent to the baker returned with two whole loaves, he hurriedly hid it away. And as soon as they had broken the bread into pieces and thrown it onto the deck, he said good night, intending to leave.

"My aunt will lock me out if I'm not back in time," he said.

Moritz and Mikael went on looking at the bear.

"Do you think it could become tame?" they asked.

Silas said he certainly thought it could—up to a point.

"It feels as if it's already a little bit ours," they said.

Silas thought of the Horse Crone and of what she would say to such a remark. He said nothing. As soon as he saw his chance, he parted from the gang and left. Now they could speculate over his presence for a couple of days, then he would return and see how they felt. Perhaps he had managed to sow a seed in their minds which would lie there and germinate by itself.

In the days that followed, Silas continued his school-

169

work with the greatest perseverance, concentratedly practicing the letters of the alphabet which the tutor had written down in his copybook and testing his knowledge on every sign that he passed. And each time he succeeded in getting a meaning out of what he read, he was filled with great satisfaction. It was like riding into new territory, he thought, like discovering strange places he had never known about.

And Fabian Fedder, who in the beginning had not been favorably disposed toward his new pupil, had to acknowledge and marvel that this same pupil's appetite for learning exceeded that of any he had encountered until then. And so it did not take long for Silas to make great strides by this perseverance, and, perhaps also because of his greater knowledge of life in general, to surpass Jorim. But, after all, Silas also thought of this period of his life as being limited. Once he had got hold of the horses again, he intended to be on his way, that was his firm resolve. . . . Meanwhile, he might as well acquire new knowledge and lay in new accomplishments to add to those he already possessed. Knowing a lot certainly never did any harm, he was sure of that.

Down in the stable the new person had started looking after the horses. This had happened without Silas having anything more to do with the matter, but Alexander Planke had taken note of the boy's information and had seen to it that the dwarf was set free. Valerian had headed straight from prison to the merchant's place and offered his services as stableboy, just as Silas had predicted. To be sure, Carnelian had grumbled about the dwarf's meager height in relation to the horses.

"Valerian," he said. "Valerian isn't a human being, it's a plant."

Tobias told Silas later that in spite of the insult the little man had certainly not been at a loss for a rebuttal. He had turned and looked the handyman straight in the eye.

"You're right," he had said. "Valerian is a flower that is one meter tall, but flowers are living things—you're nothing but a stone."

Carnelian had looked very surprised.

"And not even one of the finest at that," persevered Valerian. "A carnelian is a meat-colored, semiprecious stone."

"Where did you learn that?" Carnelian had asked eventually.

"Oh," the dwarf had replied, looking secretive, "you should not tell everything you know."

Silas stroked his chin thoughtfully when he heard that and decided that those two could have more in common than one might think offhand. Carnelian was not inclined to tell everything he knew either, and furthermore, he never said a word about himself.

But Valerian swiftly found out about Silas' evening excursions. Holding the sheepskin coat up by two fingers when Silas came in to change, he demanded an explanation.

"What is this?"

"It is the naked skin of truth," laughed Silas and then proceeded to tell him everything.

"You certainly are not timid by nature," said Valerian afterward.

171

"No," said Silas, "I've never been; it's not really in my nature. . . . And you're the only person who knows about this. Over in the master's residence the horses are never mentioned anymore; it's as if they never existed."

Valerian sighed.

"That's the way people act who have plenty," he said.

Silas shrugged and Valerian asked about the bear. "Who is looking after him?"

He was relieved when Silas told him that it was still on the barge but that a whole gang of children were taking care of it and collecting food for it.

"It's better that way," said Valerian.

"Better than what?" Silas wanted to know.

"Better than moving him somewhere else."

That Silas could agree about. Thievery was an elastic concept, and the Horse Crone would be bound to turn the bear being moved to her own advantage.

Out in the courtyard Fabian Fedder walked past, and Valerian half-squinted as he studied the household tutor's tall, stooped shape.

"Who is he?" asked the dwarf when the fellow had gone.

Silas did not know exactly what to answer; he himself knew very little about who Fabian Fedder was, except that he was the fount of book-learning available in the merchant's house. Silas had had far too much difficulty acquiring the skills of reading and writing in the short period of time that he had been in the house to concern himself with the tutor as a person. Where he went and what he did with himself when he left the merchant's house, he did not know—except for the one fact that he played in the cathedral.

"Yes, I thought as much," said Valerian.

"He wants to teach me to play the flute," said Silas.

"What did you say to that?" asked the dwarf.

"To forget about it, what else?"

The little man's much too large face acquired a grave expression.

"I would have thought you could learn that," he said.

"Learn what?"

"To play the flute. Isn't that what we're talking about?"

Silas stared at him blankly.

"In your opinion you already can play perfectly well," continued Valerian, "though you blow as the wind blows and wolves howl and rain rains down: that is not playing the flute."

"Then what is it?" asked Silas angrily.

"It's not what the tutor means in any case," said the man.

"What do you really know about this anyway?" asked Silas, feeling that the dwarf had no right to criticize him. After all, hadn't he, Silas, got this fellow out of prison?

"Well, you're right about that," replied Valerian complaisantly. Nevertheless, he had planted a worm in Silas' soul, and whether or not Silas wanted it, the worm began to feed. Deep inside he knew perfectly well that there was a difference between the way he played and the way Fabian Fedder had played in the church.

He dressed quickly and set out for the part of town by the river.

ELEVEN

Silas
and Melissa

No ONE KNEW for certain what had happened to the horses, but they had evidently been moved several times. Gradually, as the group of boys and girls became more interested in the matter, it occurred to them that information about the animals would probably not be half as easy to come by as they had thought at first, and tall Theodore was the first to give up. Anyway, he was never the one to find out anything, for he could not be bothered with the trouble of listening to people's conversations when nothing ever came of it. Moritz and Mikael saw to the eavesdropping. Their greatest merit appeared to be that they did not consider it too unmanly to work with the girls, who were generally left out when the boys became involved in any great scheme.

Of course, a few of them also saw no point in the undertaking and dropped out because they couldn't be bothered. Of those who remained, one in particular caught Silas' attention and demonstrated that she could use both her eyes and ears. Furthermore, she could put together what she had seen and heard. She was the one who had stared at Silas so angrily that first evening, and she was still not very communicative or friendly. Silas had the distinct feeling that she was observing him and very strictly assessing all the information he gave about himself. He was aware that he had to be extremely careful.

Sometimes he wondered whether she could tell that he was not what he pretended to be, but she said nothing. He just felt as if she were constantly weighing what he said against what he had said before, and, whereas the others accepted his particulars without protest, now and then he would see her mouth snap shut with every indication of disapproval. The others called her Melissa and Silas gathered that her mother worked a mangle in a laundry and her father sold firewood, but it was not so much her background that roused his curiosity as something about her manner.

He disregarded her appearance, which was no different from that of any other poor city child—the same unruly, uncared-for mop of hair and the same sallow skin—but there was something about her eyes, the way she looked at whomever she was talking to.

He was not surprised when Moritz said that she could set adults against each other. Her gaze was both steady and guarded, her questions both innocent and crafty.

That day she was irritated.

"We still don't even know where the wretched nags are," protested Moritz and Mikael simultaneously.

"But you should at least have decided who to send with the message," she said. "It'll be too late to start quarreling over that when we've got the horses."

"Well, we counted on Silas, didn't we?" the twins said defensively. "It isn't our fault that he doesn't want to go."

"You haven't asked him," insisted Melissa. She shifted her gaze from the others to Silas and he was aware of how she turned his reasons for declining upside down. He was almost certain that she did not believe him, but in no way did she reveal what her grounds for disbelief were.

"Then why don't you go yourself?" she queried, shifting her gaze back to Moritz.

"Alone?" he asked, involuntarily glancing at his brother.

"Oh well, all right then, with Mikael, it's all the same."

"One of the others would be just as good," objected Mikael.

"Yes," said Melissa, shaking the braids on her back, "but now it's too late anyway, isn't it?"

"I'm sure we can find them again," said Silas.

"If we can do it before they get sold out of town," said Melissa, thrusting her hands under her apron. "Anyway, right now I don't feel like being with you anymore because you're so slow. It's your fault that we aren't getting the reward."

177

Moritz and Mikael squirmed under her condemning eyes, which never voluntarily released their victim, and Silas was actually more involved in observing the girl than he was in being indignant that the black mare had disappeared yet again. They had traced her to an outbuilding in one of the alleys, but now she had been moved once more. Stolen goods find very little rest, he thought.

"What are you staring at?" asked Melissa, turning her head.

"You," said Silas truthfully.

"Why?"

"You're the one who should go to the merchant and demand the reward," said Silas.

She took it calmly, without blinking; she seemed to keep a perfectly straight face, yet Silas felt that he had taken her by surprise. No one would have dreamed that a girl could be sent on such an errand, least of all herself —but he could hear from the murmur that arose gradually, as the surprise subsided, that they could see the advantages perfectly. Even their breathing grew eager.

"What if I don't want to go?" she asked.

But Silas distinctly heard a challenge in her tone of voice, and he knew that she did want to; she merely wanted the others to be unanimous. None of the boys was really brave, faced with the prospect of having to venture into the wealthy part of town and having to gain admittance into the merchant's home. Melissa dared. Deep inside she wanted to. Silas realized this and kept quiet. She held her tongue about what she knew about him, so he had no reason to blurt out anything. Instead he simply shrugged.

"Oh well," he said, "there really isn't anything to go for now—the horses are probably gone."

Melissa's entire bearing expressed contempt.

"Aren't you in rather a hurry to give up?"

Silas shrugged again as if he were completely indifferent.

"Weren't you the one who thought the whole thing up?" she went on to ask. "Weren't you so clever that you knew how it should be done?"

"Quit quarreling," Mikael admonished her. "We have to find the horses again before it's too late. It doesn't matter who said what; we just have to find out where the horses are and deliver the message so that we can get the reward."

But Melissa would not be stopped, and it was to Silas that she addressed herself.

"What did you say the merchant's name was?"

Silas turned inquiringly to the twins, as if that was something they were sure to know.

"Alexander Planke," said Moritz.

"And are you sure they were his horses?"

It was still Silas whom she addressed.

"Wasn't he the one who came with the town guards that evening?" Silas asked back.

"That's no answer," said Melissa hotly.

"Well, I wasn't there, you know." Silas disclaimed both responsibility and knowledge. "I didn't see who came."

"Are you sure it was his son who rode one of the horses?" she went on.

Silas turned to the twins for help.

"Who said it was Alexander Planke's son?" he asked.

179

"Everyone," they promptly replied. "Otherwise his father surely wouldn't have paid the guard to ransack the whole neighborhood."

"Well"—Melissa half-lowered her eyelids—"then who was the other person with him?"

Silas felt as if she were drawing a net in close around him; he was convinced that she knew something. Had they been alone, he might have been able to talk with her, but as it was, he had to play his part—and she knew that. He was bound by the others' presence, and so he also passed this question on to the two brothers.

"Does anyone know who the other one was?"

There was a brief silence while each separately searched through the facts they possessed, which were nevertheless no more than guesswork.

Most of them thought he must be a brother.

"Then why do people always mention only one son of Alexander Planke?" Melissa wanted to know.

"There's something to that," said Mikael. "Well then, a friend? Some other rich man's son?"

"No other rich man came to fetch anyone in a closed coach that evening," said Melissa. "They both drove home with Alexander Planke."

"What about a servant? A groom or something?"

"In those clothes?"

Melissa's voice was sharp as a whiplash.

"Have you ever seen a groom in gentleman's clothes?" she wanted to know.

No one had. And, all things considered, no one had given any further thought as to who the other boy might be. He was like an appendage to the rich man's son.

180

"Maybe you know?" someone asked.

Melissa waited a moment before answering. She stared fixedly at Silas with narrowed eyes.

Then she asked, "Weren't you the one who talked so much about how we should find out how things fit together?"

Silas acknowledged that. Inside his head he estimated the best and fastest way to escape without having the whole horde after him. They would feel deceived now that she was about to reveal who he was.

"Some time ago there was a lot of talk about how that same rich merchant had almost driven both himself and his family to death somewhere out in the country," continued Melissa. "Do you remember that?"

There were affirmative sounds all around from the gang, but no one asked right out what that had to do with anything.

"Someone stopped that runaway four-in-hand for him by riding in at it from the side and scrambling over onto one of the lead horses. . . . Do you remember that?"

Melissa looked around inquiringly.

"Yes, people shuddered at the thought of that daring act."

"Afterward they said that he was just a big boy and that the merchant had taken him along home with him."

"Do you think he was the one?" asked Moritz and Mikael together.

"Now—what would you do if someone had saved your lives?"

"Give him something in return, of course."

181

"And if you were very rich and he was very poor?"

Melissa was talking to the twins now, but Silas still had the feeling that he was the one to whom she was directing her words. She was letting him know that he had been found out and that she had the power to reveal his presence there. With only a few words she could reveal his double life, and then what would happen?

"But do you really seriously believe that he could have been the one who was there?" asked the twins.

"Well, what do you do with someone who saved your whole family?" Melissa asked in return.

"Give him something."

"Give him what?"

"A horse?" said Silas suddenly.

Melissa's eyes met his and playfulness bubbled deep within them.

"When he already had one?" she laughed. "It would be much more appropriate to give him one now; surely one of the stolen ones was his? Do you really think the merchant would be crazy enough to want to give him another horse?"

"The merchant probably never imagined that the one he had was really his own."

Silas felt that he was skating on thin ice, but at the same time he sensed a kind of secret understanding with the girl facing him; without having budged they had drawn closer to each other.

"Then what about taking him into the house?" she asked.

"What about his parents?" Silas wanted to know.

"Do you think he has any?" She looked at him with curiosity and Silas shrugged.

182

Then he asked, "But what would a farm boy like that do in a rich man's house?"

"Good heavens, if only I were the one who had that chance!" exclaimed the girl.

The others roared with laughter.

"You!" they laughed. "How would you go about getting your foot inside the door of a place like that? Perhaps you could capture a four-in-hand?"

Melissa hesitated; the look in her eye turned crafty.

"Not a four-in-hand," she then went on, "but I really might be able to get back the two horses for Alexander Planke without your help—and wouldn't that be almost as good?"

"That would be just like you!" shouted the twins in unison. "You'd be shameless enough to do it."

Melissa swayed her hips back and forth a little in front of the others.

"Can't you just see me as a noble young lady with a parasol and a chambermaid and all the rest of it?"

"Hah," said Moritz. "You couldn't even be a chambermaid. No one would want a scarecrow like you in the house. . . . Besides, you can't find the horses again."

"No?"

Melissa swung her head to face Moritz.

"What if I already know where they are?"

"Oh come on, you don't know that."

"What do you bet?" Melissa angrily extended her hand, prepared to bet.

"We can discuss that after you've told us," Mikael broke in. "The agreement was that we would share."

"The agreement was that you would take care of sending a message when we had traced down the horses," said Melissa hotly. "And now you won't do that."

"We?"

Both Moritz and Mikael appeared infuriated. "Everyone else too."

The gang backed away from the argument and Melissa glanced at Silas, but he remained impassive.

Someone murmured, "Then you are equally to blame yourself."

"So why don't you ask if they'll take you as a chambermaid," tittered Epsi, who felt completely overshadowed by Melissa.

No one heard her.

"Who has the horses now?" asked Moritz.

Melissa looked at him calmly and solemnly.

Then she said, "Duwald Bonebreaker."

"That's a lie!" exclaimed Mikael incredulously. "As close by as that?"

"All right, go and try to see into the room behind the washhouse where he usually keeps his pig," said Melissa, unperturbed.

"Right down here in the alley?"

They could hardly believe it, for just recently they had hung around and nosed about and listened, and now it turned out that the horses were right close by. Even Epsi was astonished, and she usually knew a great deal about what Melissa was up to.

"Why would they do that?" asked Moritz. "After all, the horses were very near here to start with, and I thought they would leave town."

"They were going to," said Melissa, "but you're not

the only ones who can't agree. They were supposed to be sent away on a barge."

"How do you know that?"

"Do you think I leave my ears behind when I deliver the laundry?"

"But how do you know they are at Duwald Bonebreaker's place? You don't know that for sure, do you?"

"I heard them being brought there—last night. They passed right by our house."

"Did you follow them?"

"No, but I looked out the window. I could hear where they stopped and turned in."

"But you can't be sure that it was actually at his place." Mikael was full of doubt.

"Why else do you think there are horse droppings in his yard?"

"Did you go over there afterward and have a look?"

"My mother always buys eggs from the Bonebreakers."

"So you did see them?"

"Well, I certainly can smell the difference between pigs and horses," retorted Melissa indignantly. "You don't always have to stand staring at something to know what it is."

Silas had to control himself so as not to jump for joy; he felt a very strong urge to kick out his arms and legs and make a whole string of cartwheels. This was by far the best news he had heard in a long time.

"Why is he called Bonebreaker?" asked Silas to find out a little more about where the black mare was.

"Because he always breaks everything," said Epsi, for

once forestalling Melissa. "He broke his legs seven times."

"Nine," corrected Melissa. "And his arms at least that often. His bones are brittle and if anyone hits him something is bound to break."

"Well then surely no one hits him," supposed Silas.

"Yes, his wife does."

"That's also why he can't have a real job like other people. If he lifts anything heavy or falls down the stairs or something, he's bound to limp for a long time afterward."

"His legs are all crooked," said Epsi.

"Yes, and much too short," added Melissa. "He walks all wrong. That's also why he is never able to be in on anything. He has to be satisfied with hiding things for the others."

"Being in on what?" asked Silas.

"Robbery and things like that."

"But does he get anything for hiding things?"

"Not very much—which is why his wife beats him. The only one who dares say anything to her is that black character with the bear."

"And she's locked up," said Moritz.

"This time you had better act a little faster," said Melissa.

"We? Aren't you the one who should get going? You'd better be off right now."

"You mustn't imagine that he has time for the likes of me when he is sitting around at home," Melissa corrected them. "It should be in the morning."

"He ought to be really glad to get his horses back," someone pointed out in the back of the gang.

"But he can't know why I'm there, can he?" said Melissa angrily.

"No, but it will all work out, you're so clever," said Moritz. "As long as it's done before someone runs off with the horses again."

"Can I come along?" asked Epsi hurriedly.

"No, I want to go alone," said Melissa.

"Why?"

"Because I want to."

"That's only because you think that you can become a chambermaid," Epsi commented sourly.

"Maybe," said Melissa, "and maybe partly because you often manage to say the wrong thing."

If Mikael had not grabbed hold of Epsi from behind she would have flown at Melissa's head. As it was she had to content herself with kicking Mikael in the shin.

TWELVE

An unusual breakfast

ANNA CAME INTO the dining room and reported that a girl was standing out on the back stairs.

"A girl?" repeated the mistress in surprise.

Anna repeated the information in a voice and with an expression that disclaimed any responsibility for the disturbance.

"What does she want?" asked Mistress Elisabeth.

"To talk with the master."

Both Alexander Planke and his wife stared at the cook in astonishment. Anna knew perfectly well that they did not like to be disturbed while at table. And in the morning like this.

"I told her that," said Anna, seeing what they were thinking.

189

"But what would she like to talk to me about?" asked the merchant uncomprehendingly.

"Something important," said Anna. "She says that it is urgent."

"Tell her that we are eating."

"I have."

"Couldn't she return somewhat later?"

"If it gets to be too late, she said that the master will stand to lose," said the cook.

"Lose? . . . What kind of a girl is this? Does she work for anyone we know?"

Anna shook her head.

"I have never seen her before."

Silas remained impassive, striking the top of the shell off his egg with studied precision. Obviously this was an extremely unusual occurrence in this house.

"I don't understand," said Mistress Elisabeth. "Why can't she wait until we are finished? What can be so very urgent?"

"She will not say," said Anna, "except to the master."

"Curious," commented the merchant's wife, not knowing what to think.

"Then show her into the office and ask her to wait there a moment," said Alexander Planke, giving up, and then, addressing Japetus, he said, "Could you just go in there and hear what is so terribly urgent that we cannot even have our morning meal in peace."

Japetus obediently put down his bread and his egg spoon and left. Silas would have given a great deal to hear that exchange. It never occurred to him that she would not tell Japetus either, but seconds later Japetus

190

returned to say that she would only talk with Alexander Planke himself.

Silas looked down busily at his food.

"What kind of girl is she?" asked Ina with interest.

"I don't know; she looks quite ordinary," said Japetus.

"Can I go see her?"

"You stay right here," said Mistress Elisabeth hurriedly. "You are not finished eating."

"Neither is Japetus," grumbled Ina.

"He was told to go."

Jorim glanced from one to the other, and then slid cautiously down from his chair without a word.

"Now, now! Where are you going?"

"But I have finished," the boy defended himself.

"You will remain seated until we leave the table."

Sulkily Jorim got back up on his chair again and Alexander Planke gave instructions to inform the girl that he would like to know what this was about.

Japetus went out once more. But Silas knew Melissa well enough to know that she did not give away much information; she would not risk tipping anyone off to the whole bag of tricks prematurely. He was sure that Melissa was the right person to have been sent on such an errand.

Anna was still a thundercloud. What on earth did the girl mean by running in there at mealtime and then by not even being willing to wait? It was unheard of. It was not well-bred.

Japetus returned and said that it was about the horses. He seemed feverishly excited and he glanced at Silas repeatedly.

191

"Tell her that we have found someone to look after the horses," said the merchant indifferently. "Valerian keeps them irreproachably—whatever else you might think of him."

"I told her that, too," Japetus said. "It's not those horses."

"Which ones then?"

The merchant looked nonplussed.

"The ones that were stolen," replied Japetus.

"What does she know about that? Has she brought a message from someone?"

Japetus shook his head.

"She will not say anything more."

Alexander Planke stared straight through his son and there was no way of knowing what he saw, but his face took on a determined expression.

Then he said, "Show her in here," and began to butter himself another slice of bread.

Silas' heart leaped inside him; he felt that he was caught in the act. It would be going against the code of behavior of the house if he were to leave, and would in all probability only awaken mistrust, but at the same time he was playing into Melissa's hands by sitting there. All her conjectures would be confirmed—and what would happen if she announced that he hung around the river neighborhood every single evening when the merchant's family assumed that he was sitting up in his room reading and writing?

Mistress Elisabeth sent her husband an angry look across the table, for hadn't he agreed once and for all not to talk business while they were eating; shouldn't he think about other things occasionally, too?

The merchant nodded to her reassuringly, and Ina and Jorim settled comfortably in their chairs in expectation that now they would finally get to see the mysterious girl. She must be very remarkable since she dared face down both Anna and their father.

Silas wondered for a moment whether the merchant was doing this to show Melissa how much inconvenience she was causing, but he forgot that when Anna returned, bringing her.

Melissa stopped and curtseyed right inside the door, and the two younger children looked disappointed. She was really, as Japetus had said, quite an ordinary girl.

Alexander Planke looked at her solemnly and bit into his sausage.

Then he said, "You wanted to speak with me."

"Yes," said Melissa, casting a sideways glance at Japetus, who quietly slid back onto his chair.

Silas noted that Melissa avoided looking at the food or the table altogether, and that her hair was washed and brushed and that she was nice and neatly dressed with a clean apron.

"It's about the horses," explained Melissa.

"Which horses?" inquired the merchant.

"The ones that were stolen, of course. . . . Your horses."

"Oh yes, what about them?"

"I know where they are."

"Indeed? Where is that?"

"How much is it worth to you to know?" she asked without blinking. Silas marveled how calm she was. When he thought of how overwhelmed he himself had been those first days, it did not seem at all like the first time that Melissa had been in a house like this. The surroundings did not interest her in the slightest; only one thing occupied her seriously—her errand.

Frowning, the merchant stared at her fixedly.

"Is this extortion?" he asked right out.

Melissa smiled.

"Not at all," she said. "This is a business transaction. We have looked for the horses and found them, and now we want to sell our information. You can buy it or let it go; no one is trying to force you into anything. This is an offer—but it is urgent."

"Why?"

"They move them often, and they are sure to sell them out of town soon."

"Are you well informed?"

Melissa conceded that she was.

"And you were definitely not sent by those who stole the horses?"

Melissa shook her head so that her braids danced. Her eyes sparkled with delight.

"That would be a poor way of doing business," she laughed. "Who would ever steal two valuable horses and have the expense of keeping them stabled in different places only to deliver them back for a reward!"

Ina and Jorim stared shamelessly at the mysterious girl, but Silas got the impression that she looked at no one but the merchant himself. He also did not feel that she recognized him, but after all she had only seen him wearing his old clothes.

"We are not the people who stole them," she said.

"We?"

"Yes, there are seven of us who found them."

The merchant wanted to know what Melissa's information would cost.

"That depends on what this sort of information is worth," thought Melissa.

"And that in turn depends on whether it can be used," said the merchant.

"No," said Melissa. "We don't do business in guesswork, only in what we can answer for with certainty."

The merchant nodded appreciatively. He appeared to be well disposed toward the girl. They continued their negotiations for a good long time and then agreed on a price. Alexander counted the money out and put it down in front of him on the table. Silas was astonished to see how much it was, more than if they had sent any of the boys as a messenger, he was sure. The merchant shoved the money across to Melissa, but she did not take it.

"It has to be divided into seven shares," she demanded, glancing at the pile.

"Can't you count?" asked the merchant, surprised.

A fine blush spread over Melissa's face and she looked down.

"Not too well," she said humbly.

"But well enough to see that these coins and bills cannot be divided into seven equal shares? Have you gone to school?"

Melissa denied that. "But I deliver the laundry," she said.

"And you have learned to count from that?"

"Or else I would be cheated," the girl declared with conviction.

195

"You should go to school," observed Alexander Planke.

"I have no time; I have to help Mother with the laundry."

Alexander Planke changed the money as Melissa requested, and the girl took it and counted out a seventh of it.

Silas suddenly grew hot around the ears again, fearing that she would hand him his share on the spot. But that was not it at all. Melissa handed the money back to Alexander Planke, who looked fairly at a loss to understand her.

"What is this?" he asked.

"My share," said Melissa firmly.

"What am I to do with it?" the merchant wanted to know.

"I would like to know whether there is a position open for a chambermaid," she asked without beating about the bush.

"A chambermaid?"

Both the master and the mistress were equally taken by surprise.

"Yes, for her, for example," said Melissa, pointing to Ina, who almost fell off her chair in a flurry of confusion. "She is surely old enough to need her own maid."

Mistress Elisabeth was thunderstruck, but her husband smiled with pleasure.

"We can discuss that," he said, wiping his mouth on his napkin. "It depends on several things. First we must settle this matter of the horses. Where did you say they are?"

Melissa told him, giving a description of where the

house was and what it looked like. It was the tenth house down the street on the right-hand side, she said.

"Are you sure the horses are there?"

"They will be until tomorrow," she said. "They will be moved at the earliest in the middle of the night. People never do things like that in the day."

"You are well informed."

Melissa acknowledged that, perusing Silas with her glance. She recognized him. She had known all along that he was sitting there, and yet he would never have guessed it from the way she looked. It was a peculiar feeling.

When she had left and Anna accompanied her out to the back stairs and closed the door after them, everyone burst out talking.

Mistress Elisabeth thought that she was rather too self-assertive.

"And stubborn," said Japetus. "She was quite impossible to argue with. She simply refused to talk to me."

The merchant nodded a little to himself.

"But she also has brains in her head. I'd like to know how many of her kind are walking around not finding any use for themselves." His eyes rested thoughtfully on Ina, and his wife knew what he was considering.

"Don't you think that would be too much of a good thing?" she asked.

"What do you mean?"

"I mean for Ina. Mightn't it be too overwhelming?"

"Let us wait to decide anything until we see what happens this evening," said Merchant Planke. "We must plan how to go about this."

Both Japetus and Silas sat completely motionless

while Ina and Jorim said their thanks for the meal and left the room.

"Isn't this a matter for the town guard to handle?" asked Mistress Elisabeth. "Couldn't you just pay them for it as you did the other day?"

"I'm not sure that would be too successful," said the merchant thoughtfully.

"Successful? We got Japetus home alive. Wasn't that successful?" asked his wife.

"That was certainly not thanks to the guard, as you know full well."

"Oh, as if that little old fellow down in the stable could have had much to do with it."

"But it's true, Mother," Japetus interjected. "It was thanks to Valerian that we got free."

"You have to realize that the whole neighborhood down by the river becomes agitated and irate when the guard is sent in. It makes them band together even if they are not too well disposed toward one another otherwise. It would be ever so much better if we could solve this some other way."

"I think we can," exclaimed Silas.

"What do you mean by that, boy?"

Alexander Planke turned his head with a jerk, as if none of this could possibly concern Silas.

"Just slip me some money," said Silas, rising from his chair so fast that it scraped back over the floor.

Mistress Elisabeth stared at him disapprovingly, but Silas had no time to be respectful at that moment.

"What will you do with it?" the merchant wanted to know.

"Investigate the matter on the spot."

198

The merchant looked somewhat thoughtful. But then once again he recalled the boy's resourcefulness in stopping the four-in-hand, how he had slipped from one horse to the other and come out of it well.

"How much do you need?" he asked suddenly.

Silas named a sum which he thought would be large enough to shake the soul of any woman who was not used to seeing more than pennies.

Alexander Planke counted the sum out on the table-cloth and shoved it over to Silas without asking what he planned to do with the money.

Silas scraped the money up and galloped down to the stable on his thundering fine city shoes. And both Japetus and his parents went right over to the window expecting to see Silas reappear riding one of their best horses. But how great was their surprise when the stable door opened again and a country bumpkin with tousled hair wearing a sheepskin coat stepped out into the yard.

"Well, I never!" exclaimed Mistress Elisabeth, raising her arms to throw open the window. She would never have dreamed that Silas would be shameless enough to keep his old rags hidden when she had ordered them to be thrown out.

Her husband swiftly grabbed her wrist.

"No, stop," he said in a low voice.

"But he mustn't walk around in those clothes as long as he's living with us," protested his wife. "He mustn't be seen so vulgarly and shabbily dressed. People mustn't think that we begrudge him anything better to wear."

"Let him go," said the merchant. "I daresay he knows what he's doing."

"But where is he going?" asked Japetus.

"Where he's safest dressed like that," said his father, walking away from the window.

Japetus followed Silas with his eyes as far as he could without saying any more. Deep in his heart he felt cheated.

THIRTEEN

In Duwald Bonebreaker's house

I<small>T WAS STILL</small> fairly early in the day and the townspeople, busy with their own affairs, did not concern themselves with the boy in the sheepskin coat hurrying down the streets. People dressed in similar clothing came in from the surrounding country villages regularly to offer their wares for sale in the square, and although the clothing was unlike anything used in town, it was not unknown to the inhabitants. Silas did not feel in any way remarkable because of his appearance.

Without hesitating he hurried in the direction of the river, turning in to the winding alleyways where he had gradually become quite well known. The foul smell from thrown-out slops and excrement hung over that whole part of town, and although not all the alleys were equally nasty, he still moved with some caution.

In Ben-Godik's village people also threw out their wastes but he did not think that he could remember any comparable stench around the houses there. It must be because so many people were packed so close together here, he thought; there was too little space in the narrow gutters between the houses for the weather to carry the reek away. The lane in which both Melissa and Duwald Bonebreaker lived was somewhat wider than most of the others and for that very reason seemed to be ever so slightly cleaner. Silas slackened his pace and went past the Bonebreakers' house, walking on the opposite side of the lane and so busy observing that not particularly noteworthy building that he forgot to look where he was going and thus crashed right into a girl with an impressive basket of laundry on her arm.

It was Melissa, who at that very moment had stepped out of her mother's door. She had just come home and was still dressed as she had been that morning at Alexander Planke's. When she caught sight of Silas, she immediately thought that something had gone wrong.

"What is it?" she asked anxiously, assuming that he wanted to talk with her.

"Nothing," Silas assured her.

"Then what are you doing here?"

"Finding out something."

"What?"

"I don't know yet. Something that we can do ourselves so that we can avoid calling out the town guards."

"You mean to do with the horses?"

"If we can feel our way and act without too much commotion it would be best," said Silas.

Melissa agreed and rushed off with her basket, relieved that her trip to the merchant had not caused complications. Silas continued in the opposite direction until he reached a slightly larger intersecting street which, to all appearances, connected the river and the old quay with the inner city. A man came along pulling a handcart fully loaded with cordwood. He swung in around the corner into the alley right where Silas was standing, and Silas guessed that he must be Melissa's father on his way home to make the logs into kindling, which he would then sell in bundles for stoves.

Silas stood for a long time watching people coming and going and calling to one another across the street. Everything was very peaceful—in one place a woman, bare-legged in a pair of walked-out carpet slippers, stood talking in through an open window to another woman like herself, and a little farther down on the same side, a couple of men slipped into a tavern in spite of the early hour, and everywhere small children played on the stoops and in and out the open doors, while dogs and pigs fussed about with whatever they could find in the gutters.

A man came walking up from the river and stopped at the entrance to the lane where, far down, Melissa's father had come to a halt with his cart and was in the process of unloading the logs. Silas leaned indolently against the wall of the house without paying particular attention to the man; he was definitely from that neighborhood like all the others, and Silas was busy planning and considering what would be the best way to go about freeing the horses.

Suddenly the man turned to Silas and stared at him searchingly.

"Why are you standing here?" he asked.

Silas stopped thinking and stared back.

"I'm waiting," he said.

"Waiting? Don't you have anything to do?"

"Yes, you heard me: I'm waiting," said Silas calmly.

"For what?" asked the man, lowering his lids mistrustfully.

Silas came up with, "For my master, of course. He went over to the tavern." Silas nodded in the direction of the building where a sign indicated that it was open. "He told me to wait."

"Isn't it rather early to go to a tavern?" judged the man, continuing to stare at Silas.

"Oh well," drawled Silas, "he really does need to let off steam before he goes home to the mistress again."

The man coughed scornfully.

Then he said, "I seem to have seen you before."

"That could very well be," said Silas as casually as possible. "I have to go along every time."

"Every time?"

"Every time he goes to 'market' as he says," Silas nodded again in the direction of the tavern.

The man appeared to believe his explanation, for his tone of voice became milder.

"Would you like to earn a farthing?" he asked.

"Doing what?" asked Silas.

"Just delivering a message for me."

"I am not supposed to go anywhere," said Silas. "I have to be here when he comes out."

"Do you think he will come out right away?"

"No," said Silas. "He just went in."

"Then you can easily go."

"Is it far?" asked Silas.

"See that man with the wood cart?" asked the man, pointing down the lane.

"Is he the one?" asked Silas.

"No, the house diagonally across from him. Do you know Duwald Bonebreaker?"

Silas shook his head and the man carefully explained what the house looked like.

"You are to speak to his wife," enjoined the man.

"This Bonebreaker's wife?"

"Tell her that her brother is coming to dinner," said the man with emphasis.

"That her brother is coming to dinner," repeated Silas as if it were nothing special.

"She is to expect him just an hour after nightfall," explained the man.

Silas did not look as if he had any particular desire to walk anywhere; he remained leaning against the warm wall.

"What do I get for this?"

The man searched in his pocket, drew out a coin, and put it in Silas' hand.

"Two," charged Silas.

"Not for that short distance," objected the man.

"Then you can go over there yourself," said Silas, handing back the coin. "It's plenty for the trouble, but I need one more to lessen the pain of the thrashing I'll get if my master does come out while I'm gone and discovers that I'm not here."

The man rooted angrily around in his pocket and found one more coin which he gave Silas, whereupon they parted. Silas blessed his good fortune and set off for

Duwald Bonebreaker's house. He knocked on the door and tried the handle only to discover that it was locked. Then he tried the gate in order to get around to the kitchen door, but the gate was locked as well. Apparently no one heard him pounding.

Then he walked over to the other side of the alley, and studied the chimney, which was smoking quite splendidly. He concluded that someone must be home even if not a sound could be heard. But since the man had not given him any instructions as to how he should get in, only what to say, Silas had to figure out something. He both had to and wanted to get inside. He stepped up onto the windowseat determinedly and grabbed hold of the low roof and when he was finally up on the roof it was a small matter for him to persevere on up to the roof ridge and from there down the other side. Halfway down he stopped and hunkered down to look around. Behind the house was the open yard and behind the yard lay a low, dilapidated outbuilding, which could be the washhouse that Melissa had mentioned. If so, the horses were inside. A greenish, rotten fence separating the yard from the other neighboring yards formed one side of the washhouse.

Silas looked beyond the washhouse roof down into an overgrown back garden that must belong to a house facing out onto the next alley.

He slid down the last part of the roof and landed light as a cat outside the kitchen window, where a terrified woman's face immediately appeared. It was definitely not every day, thought Silas, that someone dropped in from the roof. At least the face did not exactly look as if it expected guests from that quarter.

As soon as the woman saw that it was only a boy and therefore not dangerous, she came streaking out the kitchen door and set upon Silas in the roughest way before he could manage to get out any explanation as to who he was or why he had come or why he had entered the way he did. Her abusive outburst was so persistent that Silas gave up trying to interrupt and instead prepared himself to wait until it finally came to an end. She shouted so loudly that old Bonebreaker himself came limping from his outbuilding on his crooked pins to hear why she was making such a racket. He evidently thought that he was the one who had incurred his wife's wrath by doing something wrong and he brightened up considerably when he discovered Silas and realized that the boy was the culprit. Very cheerful, he hobbled right up to Silas, who had sat down on the ground defiantly until the storm passed. He did not feel the slightest bit contrite, as well he might according to the woman.

"What were you doing on our roof?" she asked finally, going all the way out into the yard and looking up at the chimney as if she expected to find several others up there.

"Coming in," said Silas.

"Why didn't you go to the door like everyone else?"

"Because it was locked."

"That didn't give you permission to push your way in by the roof."

"Yes," insisted Silas.

"You say yes?"

The woman was speechless, dumbfounded by his insolence, and the Bonebreaker himself stood gloating.

They had never seen the likes of this fellow in the place before.

"I have a message," said Silas.

"From whom?" the woman wanted to know.

"I was to bring greetings from your brother," said Silas, observing how the Bonebreaker's wife's expression suddenly changed from ill will to deep interest.

"You fool, why didn't you say that right away?" exclaimed the woman. "Come on in."

Silas rose and the woman shoved him straight toward the door with small, eager prods of her fingertips.

"How did you expect him to be able to do that," asked the Bonebreaker, "the way you were carrying on?"

"Shut up," snarled the woman.

"But he's right," Silas came to the man's rescue.

"Now now, no impertinence," ordered the woman, shoving him all the way into the kitchen. The Bonebreaker kept close at their heels as if he were afraid of being shut out.

"Now then, what was it?" asked the woman.

"Well," started Silas, sniffing the kitchen aroma. Then he said, "Ah, it smells good here," looking over at the stove where a jug of batter and a plate of pancakes showed what the woman had been doing when he fell from the roof so unexpectedly.

"It certainly is a long time since I had anything to eat," announced Silas.

"Give him a pancake," urged the Bonebreaker.

"Stop butting in," bade his wife.

"But he's starving," added the man, sniffing the aroma pleasurably himself.

208

"At least let me buy a couple," said Silas, getting out one of the small coins which he had been given for taking the message. "It's ages since I had pancakes."

The woman devoured the coin greedily with her eyes and took down a plate while the Bonebreaker pushed his way in onto the bench beside Silas expectantly.

"You might as well save yourself the effort," said his wife.

"You can have one of mine," murmured Silas, thinking that it might prove useful to become good friends with the man of the house.

"Who said that you can have two?" asked the woman caustically.

"I did," said Silas, "and that's not one bite too much."

Scowling, the woman flung two pancakes onto the plate and shoved them over to Silas, who poured a heap of sugar on them and signaled to the Bonebreaker that one pancake was for him. Duwald threw himself upon the food with a triumphant sidelong glance at his wife.

"See this, Martha?" he chuckled. "Here I am sitting like a guest in my own kitchen."

"Your own?" The woman instantly flared up. "Is there anything here that you could call your own?—except those very bad bones of yours."

The Bonebreaker ducked and hastily crammed the last bite into his mouth as if he expected her to snatch it away from him. He sat there quivering with pleasure, protected by the unknown messenger's presence. Now and then he mumbled something to himself. Only when Silas had finished chewing did the woman come over and plant herself in front of him with her arms akimbo.

"Well?" she exhorted him.

"That tasted good," conceded Silas.

"Now what are you supposed to say?"

"Thank you for the food," said Silas politely.

"Oh shut up!" yelled the woman. "I mean the message, of course."

"Oh yes," Silas remembered, "there was that message, wasn't there? It was tremendously important, from what I could understand."

He handed the empty plate to the woman, but she pretended not to see it.

"Well, what was it?" she asked.

"My stomach is growling so loudly that I can't remember," said Silas solemnly.

"Nonsense."

"Won't you give me one pancake just to know what it is?" he asked with an innocent expression.

The woman flung a pancake onto his plate ill-temperedly.

"Two," ordered Silas.

"You said one," said the woman.

"One for each of us, of course."

Yet another pancake landed on the plate and Silas and the Bonebreaker wolfed them down, united in silence.

"Now what was it about my brother?" the woman wanted to know.

"He wants to come," said Silas, glancing at the heavy iron skillet she stood holding. Good heavens, did she ever put that down with a bang!

"When?"

"To dinner."

"Are you sure?" she said, taken by surprise.

210

"No," said Silas.

"Then why did you say it?"

"Because that's what he said; I'm only repeating it, so I can't be sure that he will really turn up."

He shot a glance at the pancakes but the woman pursed her lips with a tight movement that turned down any requests.

"How many brothers do you have?" he asked instead, fishing the other small coin from his pocket and starting to play with it on the table.

The woman stiffened watchfully at his question, and Silas felt her weighing how much he might know. Evidently the number of "brothers" was not something that was set.

"Why?" she asked without replying.

He merely shoved the coin across the table. So there are more than one, he thought. On the other hand, more than two would look strange moving a pair of horses, for that would attract attention.

"I just wondered whether there might be a couple more pancakes for me," said Silas meekly.

The woman bit her lips and for the third time brought two pancakes from the stove and flung them onto his plate.

"Did he say anything about why he wanted to come so early?" she wanted to know.

Silas delayed saying no and pretended to ransack his memory.

She tried to help him along. "Did he name anyone else?"

"No—" Silas still hesitated, dragging the time out.

"Did he say anything about a rich merchant?" she added.

"No, now that he did not say, I'm sure," Silas assured her.

The Bonebreaker's wife was about to ask something else—she had already opened her mouth—when she closed it again abruptly and fell silent. Silas would have given a great deal to know what the horse thieves feared so much that they were willing to venture out so early with stolen goods. He finished chewing politely and rose.

"I have to go now," he said.

The woman did not look as if she wanted to detain him, but the Bonebreaker mumbled on at length about how it had been a great pleasure.

Silas coolly told the story of his master who was sitting in the tavern waiting for him.

"Do you hear that, Martha?" said the Bonebreaker. "Someone who can go to the tavern—even at this early hour of the day."

"Shut your mouth," snarled the woman.

"Do you like beer?" grinned Silas.

Duwald smacked his lips noisily.

"Go on out now and open the gate so that he can be on his way," said his wife sourly.

The Bonebreaker obeyed automatically; he drew Silas with him out into the yard and around into the entry where he began to remove a huge iron bar so that the small door in the middle of the gate could be opened.

"Would you like a mug of brandy?" whispered Silas, while a plan began to dawn on him.

The Bonebreaker forgot what he was doing and stared at Silas with huge round eyes.

"How could that be managed?"

"I could bring it to you."

"But, dear me, I have no money at all," the man wailed, shuffling his unequally long legs.

"But I do."

Silas showed him one of the heavy coins that he had got at the breakfast table. Back then he had thought that he would bribe the Bonebreaker's wife to let the horses out, but, having seen her, he did not dare rely on her. He would certainly have more success with the Bonebreaker himself.

"Then am I to stand here and wait?" asked Duwald uncertainly.

"No, go down to your outbuilding and I'll slip it in to you over the fence," said Silas.

The Bonebreaker beamed like a watchman's lantern and he almost locked up on Silas' heels from pure eagerness. What a day—first pancakes and then brandy!

"No, wait!" said Silas. "First you have to tell me which gate to use to get in from the next alley."

"Oh, that's easy," the lame man assured him. "You can't go wrong; a wheelwright lives there."

Silas hurried off; mornings like these went confoundedly fast and he still had so much to do. Over at the tavern he bought not a mug but a whole stone jug of brandy which he thrust under his coat and when he came out, there stood Melissa out of breath waiting for him. She must have seen him and run after him.

"I just wanted to say that she is free now," gasped the girl.

"Who is free?" asked Silas, adjusting the jug with a shove.

"Her, the black one with the bear, what did you call her?"

"The Horse Crone?"

"I met her; she was in a terrific hurry; she must be down at the barge by now."

Silas let out a thin, expressive whistle like a flute.

"Ah ha," he said, "so that is why they are moving the horses so soon."

"What?" asked Melissa.

"They're moving them earlier," said Silas, "at dinner time."

"Why?"

"We'll find out. You run home and keep an eye on what happens."

Melissa would have liked to learn more, but when she saw that he was busy and in a hurry, she rushed home again, while Silas headed into the wheelwright's lane where he found the correct gate. And since it was open and since there was no one in sight anywhere, he walked in and went right on down into the back garden to the neglected apple trees, where the Bonebreaker was already waiting, squeezed in a corner by the rotten fence. Silas handed him the jug and smiled to see how the man's face twitched with joy and how he hugged the brandy to himself as if it were a little baby. Never had he known the likes of this wonderful day. He hurried off into his washhouse and Silas could vividly picture him settling down close to the two horses he was supposed to guard.

Silas examined the wooden fence and found a place

where a rather large piece could be pried loose, and without a second thought, he broke the posts off close to the ground and propped them loosely back in place with the use of a brace.

Then he hurried back to the Bonebreaker's house and banged on the door and this time he was heard: The woman's head appeared in one window and when she saw who it was she quickly opened up.

"What is it now?" she asked anxiously.

"A new message from your brother," said Silas, digging a big, heavy coin from his pocket as proof. The woman's eyes bugged open and she understood very clearly that something serious must be in the works.

"I am to say that the bear trainer is free and that under no circumstances should you open up as long as she is in the neighborhood."

That was a shot in the dark, but he did see her start when he mentioned the Horse Crone. People around here didn't like her and what is more it even looked as if they were frightened of her.

"Keep the door and the gate locked whatever happens," he said, placing the coin in the woman's hand. She did not look particularly pleased at the thought of what lay in store for her.

But then Martha Bonebreaker pressed her lips together with determination and closed her fist firmly around the large coin, and Silas left her house to hurry back to the merchant's residence as best he could. It was already fairly late and the Horse Crone was definitely not one to keep people waiting.

FOURTEEN

With cunning and caution

Silas did not take the time to go see Alexander Planke in his office or in the warehouse or wherever else he might be; what had to happen now had to happen fast and he could not wait for instructions from anyone. Instead, he rushed right over to the stable to get hold of Valerian and learn whether, at some earlier point in time, the Horse Crone had thought that she too might share some of the profits from the stolen horses. Then afterward he had to find Carnelian and Tobias. Not because he thought Tobias had any particular desire to participate in the return of the horses—he had already completely left his job in the stable—but perhaps he could be persuaded to come along for Merchant Planke's sake. They had to act on their own, even though the merchant always emphasized that he and he alone made the decisions. Even Tobias would have to understand that.

Silas opened the stable door and stopped short, startled in the deepest place within his soul, for wasn't Tobias standing in his old clothes way down at the other end by the tack room talking with Valerian? Silas could not hear what they were saying, but their voices had that dogged tone that voices develop when each party holds to his own opinion equally uncompromisingly.

But why had Tobias been moved back to work here?

After all, Silas had heard only words of praise for the new shop clerk, so why was he standing here arguing with Valerian? And Valerian was certainly doing a marvelous job looking after the horses.

The dwarf raised his arm imploringly and pointed down the stable to Silas. Tobias, who stood facing him with his back to the door, swung around and turned out to be Japetus.

Silas was dumbfounded.

Japetus was dressed in the former stableboy's cast-off clothes. It was almost unbelievable; Silas stared at the merchant's son.

"I want to come along this evening," insisted Japetus, still using the same tone as before, implying that he had already discussed the matter with Valerian for a very long time and that Valerian, equally constantly, held to the opposite view.

"That is reckless and unjustifiable," said Valerian.

"But after all, I was along when the horses were lost, so it is only reasonable that I take part in bringing them back," said Japetus.

"Where is Tobias?" asked Silas.

"He has no time," declared Japetus curtly.

"So he loaned you his clothes instead?"

"He did not; I bought them."

"Bought?"

"I had to."

Japetus' voice turned gloomy at the thought of that transaction.

"It sounds as if you had to pay dearly," said Silas casually.

"He knew perfectly well that I couldn't get things like this anywhere else, at least not so quickly."

"Why couldn't he be the one to come along; I've been counting on him," said Silas.

"Then I could stay and weigh flour instead, I suppose," said Japetus bitterly. "Why can't anyone understand that I want to come along tonight?"

Silas became aware of how very important this was to Japetus.

So he said, "You won't have to wait until night. The horses will be moved somewhere else as early as dinner time and we have to be terrifically fast on our feet to get there first."

Both Japetus and Valerian promptly forgot their quarrel and both at once began to fire questions at Silas, who explained briefly what he had experienced during the course of the morning.

"Has the bear trainer ever laid any claim to the horses?" Silas asked, addressing his question to Valerian.

"She has indeed!" He grinned. "She said that they were hers—hers and hers alone—because she was the one who saw to it that the two of you were detained while the others took the horses away—but she can't get much out of that claim as long as she's sitting in the jug. The constable must have a whole lot to discuss with her."

Valerian rubbed his hands together, satisfied by the knowledge that the Horse Crone was well installed for a long time to come.

"She's out now," said Silas, watching the color drain from the dwarf's face.

"How do you know that?" he almost whispered.

"Melissa has seen her."

"Then it's urgent," came Valerian's decisive comment. "And I'm really in trouble."

"You don't want to come along?"

"I mean afterward. She won't be able to endure the fact that I have done well, that I've got around her and found work. She considers that she owns me the way you own an ape or some other animal."

"But she can't hold you against your will, can she?" Silas asserted, since after all Valerian was not a child like Jef.

"I wouldn't put anything past her," murmured Valerian despondently. "Besides, she is so awesomely strong."

"Well, in my opinion, I think you're rather good in terms of strength yourself," said Japetus, referring to the time Valerian threw him down on the deck and held him there. "I was both black and blue afterward."

Valerian smiled lopsidedly.

"That's nothing compared with her," he said sadly.

"But where is Carnelian?" Silas wanted to know.

"We have to find Carnelian in a hurry. Does anyone know where he is?"

"Here." The sound issued from the loft. Then the handyman's long legs poked out of the hatch through which hay was forked.

"Were you listening?" asked Valerian indignantly.

Silas was sure that Valerian had not intended Carnelian to overhear the fact that he was somewhat frightened of the Horse Crone.

"With wonder and delight," admitted Carnelian, landing on the floor.

Valerian glared at him.

"It's actually the first time I have heard the young gentleman express a will of his own," he added.

Japetus blushed discreetly and Valerian's expression became gentler.

"And now to the point," continued Carnelian. "What should we take with us?"

"Ourselves," said Silas, "and plenty of speed."

For the last time Valerian muttered something about irresponsibility, but no one listened to him.

"Shall we ride or drive?" asked Carnelian.

Silas thought it over.

Then he said, "I think we should walk. We'll attract less attention, and we have to move cautiously if we're to succeed."

Japetus marveled how deftly Silas took them the fastest way through town and how well he knew that neighborhood where the streets were nothing but crooked alleyways. Never for an instant was he in doubt as to how to proceed nor did he lead them directly to the

Bonebreaker's house as they had naturally expected but to the wheelwright's gate instead, where he had taken in the brandy jug unhindered.

This time it would not go so smoothly, for an unbelievable commotion over in the Bonebreaker's lane had caused the wheelwright to plant himself out in his yard even though he could see nothing of what was happening from there. But when he caught sight of the troop turning into his entryway, he could only believe that they were some of the commotion-makers and that they had something to do with the disturbance over in the other alley.

"Please be so good as to leave," he said, trying to shoo the four of them out the gate. "I don't want to get involved," he said.

"But we only want to—" Silas attempted.

"I will not allow anyone in here!" shouted the wheelwright.

"Well, Dad, that's not for you to decide," said Carnelian calmly, stepping right up to the furious man.

But the wheelwright bellowed and fenced with his arms and would not budge.

"You're making it worse for yourself," said Carnelian. "If you don't stop all this shouting we'll have to make you be quiet, and that isn't apt to be very pleasant."

The wheelwright fell silent, puzzled and perturbed.

"You would be wise to go into your house and act as if you can neither hear nor see," continued Carnelian.

Silas opened the door from the gate into his workplace and walked over to a large pile of wood shavings.

"See here," he said to the wheelwright, who, sizzling with suppressed rage and indignation, had followed him,

222

"you may well have to build yourself another fence; the old one is rotten."

The wheelwright gave a start as Silas turned his pocket inside out and let an unknown number of coins fall into the wood shavings.

"Now sit down here and be nice and quiet and count them," said Silas.

The wheelwright stared at his shavings fixedly, unaware that Silas left and closed the door behind him.

Down in the back garden under the untended fruit trees, they could distinctly hear the din from the next alley and Silas was somewhat comforted to know that whatever might be happening was taking place outside the Bonebreaker's house. Inside everything was silent and still.

Together with the others he hurriedly removed the section of fence that he had loosened that morning, thus creating a usable opening into Duwald Bonebreaker's yard right next to his washhouse. Silas cautiously slipped in and opened the door. To his great dismay the little room was chock-full of chickens which, terrified by his sudden appearance, flapped about, shrieking and cackling up to the ceiling and out through the door. There was no way that Silas could possibly squeeze in before most of them had spread out into the yard, more and more, on and on, flapping and flapping, some running out with outstretched necks. Only when there were no more left did he have an opportunity to go in and look around.

It was clearly a long time since any washing had been done there, he thought; the whole floor was covered with straw; along one wall stood a row of breeding coops

223

several stories high—though the huge copper tub was still there and pots hung on big nails in the wall.

But all the chickens?

Were they supposed to prevent unwelcome people from going into the back room? Was it always like this, or only now that the horses were there? Whatever the case, no stranger could enter without letting the chickens get out, that he had seen. Perhaps the Bonebreaker himself could manage to do it because they knew him. Silas looked out the door to where the chickens had settled down in the yard and immediately set about scratching in the rubbish heap. Nothing indicated that the Bonebreaker's wife inside the house had discovered what had happened; she was undoubtedly totally preoccupied by events out in the lane, whether she was arguing with someone through the closed windows or hunching down in the corner from fear. Duwald the Bonebreaker himself must be guarding the horses alone.

Silas opened the door to the back room. Just as he had expected, the Bonebreaker sat comfortably relaxed with his back against the wall and his legs stretched out in the straw in front of him—as well as they could be stretched considering their crookedness. His head was bent forward; it rested heavily on his chest and a loud snore indicated what he was up to. But he still held his hands protectively around the clay jug which was propped up in the straw in front of him.

"You certainly didn't take your time over that," murmured Silas, untying the dapple, turning it carefully so that it wouldn't step on the sleeping man. After all, there was no reason to inflict more injuries on him—his sturdy wife would undoubtedly see to that herself.

As silently as possible he led the horse out. He could hear both pounding and kicking on the gate and the sound of horses' hoofs might add to the frenzy of whoever was standing out there wanting to get in. Slowly he eased the dapple out through the hole in the fence. Japetus came forward to receive it but Silas went on past him and handed the animal over to Carnelian.

"But shouldn't I—?" exclaimed Japetus, both disappointed and offended.

"No," said Silas, "this one Carnelian will take."

Japetus sulked, not understanding the arrangement, since this was the horse that he usually rode, but Silas gave no further explanation. The commotion in front of the gate told him that time was short and he hurried back for the mare, which he also managed to bring out and lead through the fence into the wheelwright's back garden.

Now it can't end in total disaster, he thought, handing the reins to Valerian, who looked completely confused.

"Carnelian can give you a foot up if it's difficult," said Silas.

Valerian recovered.

"I'm not so decrepit that I can't still manage that myself," he declared. But he did not reach very high, standing next to the long-legged mare.

"What about me?" asked Japetus with ill-concealed resentment.

"You stay right here," said Silas.

"Here?"

"Yes, with me. Carnelian and Valerian can ride the horses back to your father's house. You'll help me."

"With what?"

"Well, we can't leave that there, can we?" asked Silas, pointing to the destroyed fence.

Carnelian and Valerian protested as well; they considered that they could all leave since they had paid the wheelwright and surely that was enough.

Silas stuck to his opinion.

"Then couldn't we wait for you?" asked Carnelian.

"No, ride off. If you feel like it, you can come back and see what is happening over on the other side, but first the horses should go home."

Valerian grasped the mane firmly with both hands and was instantly seated triumphantly on the horse's back unaided. Carnelian still protested.

"What do you think will happen if the gate swings open and they find you standing here with the horses?" Silas finally asked.

Then at last the handyman gave in and followed Valerian out through the wheelwright's gate. As soon as they were gone, Silas and Japetus began to put the fence back in place so that it would look functional, at least from inside the Bonebreaker's yard.

Then Silas went into the hen house with Japetus following him.

"Phew! What a stench!" gasped the merchant's son.

"To hell with that, you can hold your nose some other time. Now come over here and help."

Silas stood over the sleeping man. Japetus was totally perplexed when he found out that a man was there, moreover one who appeared to be lifeless.

"Who is it?" he asked in a whisper.

"The man who lives here."

"Is he dead? Have you—did you have to—?"

226

"You mean did I have to kill him to get the horses out?"

Silas looked cheerfully at Japetus, who had turned quite pale.

"He's drunk," he informed Japetus, as he said nothing.

"Grab hold of him here," he went on, removing the jug, which was not completely empty. "We'll put him all the way over by the wall."

"Why?"

"So they won't find him when they come crashing in now."

Japetus did not understand all this solicitude for a stranger, especially such a common man who smelled of brandy and chicken shit and who had the effrontery to keep their horses locked up.

"Do you happen to know him?" he asked.

"Oh yes," said Silas. "We ate pancakes once off the same plate."

"Spread some of this over him," he added, pulling some straw down from the loft above.

He himself spread a thick layer out over where the horses had stood, covering every trace of the big animals apart from the rings on the wall to which they had been tethered.

"Fine," said Silas, walking back into the first room. "Now all that's left are the chickens."

"You can't possibly mean that they have to be brought back inside?" asked Japetus.

"Of course," replied Silas cheerfully.

"How in the world will you ever manage that? The whole yard is full of them!" asked Japetus, worriedly glancing at the scratching, clucking flock spread out clear over to the house.

"You just go where they can't see you," said Silas. "They're frightened of strangers."

Japetus planted himself obediently over in the angle between the washhouse and the destroyed fence and listened to how Silas noisily removed the cover from the grain bin in the corner.

Immediately the nearest hen raised her head and looked attentively in the direction of the sound.

"Chick, chick, chick," Silas called softly from inside while gently tapping the grain scoop against the feed trough. This was more than the chickens could stand; the nearest ones strolled grandly in through the door and started gobbling the grains while pecking their beaks against the feed trough to summon an even greater number to congregate. The sound of eating itself drew them all in, and Silas poured out more grain. At last he tossed a couple of full scoops through the doorway into the other room where the grains fell with a rattling sprinkle down into the straw.

Instantly a whole flock flew after them, obviously not used to so much food at one time, and they fell upon it, while Silas moved around along the wall so as not to scare them. The yard was now entirely empty except for a couple of laggards who came dashing all the way from the kitchen door.

When they were well and truly inside, Silas shut the door quietly after them and looked around for Japetus.

"Well, I'll be damned!" said the latter, stepping out from his hiding place.

228

"You can really see what would have happened if we'd started to run around chasing them," said Silas.

"Yes," said Japetus, listening to the noise from the alley.

"Shall we go out and see what's happening?" said Silas, grinning.

"Are you crazy?" exclaimed Japetus, who had assumed that they would simply go back out through the wheelwright's gate. He did not fancy such a mob of angry, wildly excited people, and he knew all too well what they thought of people from the wealthier part of town.

"But no one will know you," objected Silas.

Japetus looked down at himself and acknowledged that his clothes bore very little resemblance to the clothes that he had worn when they were caught by the Horse Crone and thrown into the hold of her barge.

"How will you ever get out of here?" he asked. "You don't intend to go over and open the gate?"

"Through the neighbor's gate," said Silas. "Or, if that is locked too, through the neighbor's neighbor's gate. That's no problem. I guarantee you that all the yards are empty now."

Without asking any further questions, Japetus followed Silas in over the fence to the yard next door and from there into the adjoining one. Without waiting for anyone to come open up for them and let them out, Silas removed the iron bar and opened a door through the wall.

The hubbub and shouting were suddenly very nearby.

FIFTEEN

The Horse Crone and the horse thieves

SILAS POKED HIS head out through the opening in the wall and looked around. What a crowd! They had come out at the back of the crowd; it was impossible to see what was actually happening, but that something or other was taking place right in front of the Bonebreaker's house there was no doubt.

Without waiting for Japetus, Silas slipped out through the little door and started worming his way into the gathering. Japetus closed the door and plunged in after him as best he could, doggedly, seldom looking at the people he touched. They were not the sort he was used to, and he could not help being somewhat frightened; he knew so little about their way of life, and their crude shouts took him by surprise every time. Therefore he was anxious not to lose sight of Silas, for Silas would know what to say if they turned on him as a stranger.

Somewhere in the confusion they ran into Melissa.

"Where are you going?" she asked Silas.

"Over to see what they're up to," he supposed.

"Don't bother. You've come too late," she said, inspecting Japetus in his unaccustomed clothes.

"Too late for what?" Silas wanted to know.

"To get the horses. The bear trainer is standing right over there."

"Oh," said Silas.

"Why do you say 'oh'? Do you imagine that you two are a match for her?" Melissa looked at Silas scornfully with widening eyes. "But that would suit you perfectly, wouldn't it? Besides, the others are over there too."

"What others?"

"The thieves. The ones who hid the horses with Duwald."

"Oh," said Silas, and Melissa could not understand why what she told him made so little impression.

"And Martha, the Bonebreaker's wife, won't open up," she went on. "She says that they don't have any horses and that it's a lie that Duwald was given money to keep them hidden. That all they have are chickens."

"She's right about that," concurred Silas.

"What are you saying?"

"She's right; they don't have any horses."

"Oh yes they do. Where else would they have gone? I was in fetching eggs early this morning and they were there; I could hear them."

"Still, she's right to insist that there aren't any horses there now—she just doesn't know that herself."

"Tell me, do you think I'm standing here lying right in your face?" shouted Melissa indignantly.

Silas smiled gently at the girl.

"You just don't know any better," he said.

Japetus did not care for the conversation; he felt it must be wrong to stand saying things like this right in the middle of a whole crowd of strangers. If someone heard them and realized what they were talking about, they could be accused on the spot.

"Then where are they?" asked Melissa skeptically.

"In Merchant Planke's stable," said Silas right out.

"Oh, that's a lie," judged Melissa incredulously. "I've been sitting at the window ever since I spoke to you this morning. I never saw them come out."

"That's because you can't see around corners," teased Silas.

"Is that a fact?" said Melissa, offended. "Are there that many corners between our windows and the Bonebreaker's house, may I ask?"

"They came out into the other alley, through the wheelwright's yard."

"But there's no gate in the fence," Melissa replied, frowning.

"No, but there was for a while."

"Is it true?" Melissa asked Japetus with a look of relief.

He merely nodded. Didn't like the conversation. Instead he asked whether they might go over and see what was happening. It sounded as if someone was kicking the Bonebreaker's gate.

"She is," explained Melissa.

"Then she got here first?" asked Silas.

Melissa nodded.

Silas pushed his way on through the crowd with Melissa and Japetus following him, without stopping until they could not only hear the sound of the Horse Crone's iron-spiked boots against the gate but see them as well. She was determined to get in. The two legitimate thieves who had come to move the horses to safety could only watch. They had long since given up quarreling with the woman; they could not possibly make her comprehend that their right to the horses was greater than hers.

"That's because she failed to get the ransom money for us," murmured Silas.

Half-asleep, the bear sat beside the Horse Crone. It looked bored, and indeed it had been sitting there for a long time already. But even though it looked very peaceful, no one dared go too close. It moved only when the gate gave way and fell—not in, as might have been expected, for the bar was still in place, but out—so that both the Horse Crone and the bear had to jump to one side.

A murmur passed through the gathering, which suddenly could see into the yard behind, and Martha Bonebreaker's careworn face floated white and anxious in a window—and then her "brothers," the two horse thieves, of whom Silas recognized one at least, immediately stepped in over the pieces of broken planks and were on their way over to the Bonebreaker's outbuilding.

Gradually as the gate began to yield they had moved closer, and now they made use of the confusion to get there first.

The Horse Crone snorted and fumed with fury and stormed after the thieves, accompanied by the bear, but even at her frantic pace she could not overtake them.

"I'll be damned!" murmured Silas, striding after them.

"About what?" asked Japetus.

"She's taking the bear in to the horses."

"But you said they weren't there," said Melissa.

"She doesn't know that."

"Yes, that's really strange," said Japetus, stopping inside the gate.

"She's forgotten," Melissa supposed, "or else she thinks she can hold it with one hand and the horses with the other."

She was right behind the thieves when they reached the washhouse and threw open the door and crashed in —and doubled up and staggered back with their arms up over their heads to protect themselves from the chickens, whose terror reached unsuspected heights at the sight and smell of the bear outside. Like screeching, flapping feather balls they rose up into the air as high as they could, landing mainly on the roof where, still screeching and flapping, they ran up until they reached the roof ridge. There they shook themselves, and those that were cocks began to crow as if they had performed great feats.

Meanwhile the men went on into the back room— and came out again with a different look on their faces, calling for Martha.

"But I did say that there were no horses there," the woman insisted over and over.

They took her by the arm and shook her.

"Where is Duwald?" they demanded to know.

The Bonebreaker's wife looked at them in a daze. How should she know where Duwald was?

"But I did say—" she repeated tonelessly.

They shook her.

"He must have taken them with him," she explained, as if she had just woken up. "He went off with them."

"Where?"

"How should I know?" wailed the woman in terror.

"I'll burn the house down over your head if you don't tell," declared the Horse Crone.

"No, you won't," stated Silas calmly.

"What do you know about that?"

The Horse Crone spun halfway round and examined the speaker.

"I can set fire to the whole neighborhood if I feel like it," she continued.

"It wouldn't pay to do that," judged Silas.

She stared at him searchingly.

Then she said, "You mean you know where the horses are?"

"Yes," said Silas.

"Of all the devil's brood you're the worst," she burst out savagely.

Silas bowed.

"You're the one who took them away," she went on. "I know you well."

Japetus tugged at Silas' arm anxiously, but Silas merely smiled. Though she remembered him from before, she did not recognize him as the boy she had trussed and floored in the hold of her barge.

"Well, where are they?" she wanted to know.

"Where they should be," said Silas.

"And where is that?"

"In Alexander Planke's stable."

That was the last place anyone present could have imagined. Everyone knew that the horses came from Merchant Planke's place originally, but everyone also knew that he had long since given up trying to get them back. A deep gasp of surprise rose from the crowd, while both the thieves and the bear trainer stared at Silas in disbelief.

"You wily fox!" exclaimed the latter. "You're the one who pinched them!"

"Pinched?" repeated Silas questioningly.

"Dirty thievery of the worst kind," continued the Horse Crone. The Bonebreaker's wife's "brothers" approached menacingly.

"You can't really say that it is thieving if the horses are returned to their rightful owner," stated Silas. "Besides, one of them was mine."

"The devil take you! You thieving rascal! Perhaps you know what people do with someone like that around here."

"I suppose people give them pancakes," said Silas undaunted.

"No, people hang them out in the canal with their heads down."

"Have you tried it?" Silas wanted to know.

The Horse Crone slowly raised one yellow finger and pointed spitefully at Japetus.

"Was he the one riding the other horse?" she asked.

"Do you think he looks like that?" asked Silas, smiling. "Do you think Alexander Planke sends his well-bred son out to catch horses? I think he looks much more like a stableboy."

Japetus felt ill-at-ease there even though Silas concealed his birth, nor did Melissa feel safe so close to the dark woman with the bear. In her disappointment that the horses were safely beyond her grasp, she might very well think of taking revenge. Her threat of starting a fire might not be so empty now after all. The fear of fire was very great in that densely populated part of town.

"Shouldn't we go?" whispered Melissa. "I can't stand being here any longer."

Silas thought of the man in the washhouse lying in the straw with the jug. He would not have a very pleasant time either if he were suddenly discovered now. It might easily cost his frail, feeble body another couple of fractures if both the horse thieves and the Horse Crone were to vent their wrath on him. His wife had long since fled into the house, closing the door and probably locking it behind her, and the crowd that had pushed its way into the yard in the hope of being entertained by a tremendous fight had to face the disappointment that nothing would come of it. To be sure, the bear trainer and Martha Bonebreaker's two "brothers" scowled ominously at each other and lashed out with abusive words. Not one of them wanted to be the first to leave the battlefield. Silas also had the feeling that the Horse Crone was waiting for something, and he knew her well enough to know that her act of revenge would be lightning-fast and absolutely ruthless. He really wanted her out of the yard before Duwald Bonebreaker woke up.

Silently he slipped the flute out from his coat and

started to play for the bear, who was sitting on its back-side staring intently at the chickens on the roof. The general bickering did not interest it. But music did. It stood right up and came straight over to Silas—and went on coming even though the Horse Crone rattled its chain and grabbed hold of it again. The sounds that Silas produced were stronger than the hand that held the brightly polished chain, and the Horse Crone could only choose between following or letting go.

She chose the first.

To let go of the animal was to lose her only protection, and the two glowering men, who were perfectly justified in thinking it was her fault that the horses had disappeared, did not wish her well.

Silas walked out through the gate playing the flute, heading straight down the alley in the direction of the canal and the river, and the people, who for a moment had felt somewhat cheated because no real confrontation had taken place after Duwald's outbuilding had been broken into, immediately eyed new entertainment.

"She should be thrown into the water!" they shouted. "Chuck her out into the canal."

Only one person shouted at first, but the cry caught on. There was no doubt that the Horse Crone was dis-liked and did not belong there. No one tried to defend her; everyone wanted her out in the canal.

How they imagined that it could be done was a mystery to Silas, but he thought that no such drastic measures were necessary, just as long as they got rid of her.

"You little devil!" the Horse Crone hissed at Silas over the bear.

He half-turned and smiled at her powerless rage.

She believes that she will be drowned, he thought. She definitely believes that she will be thrown into the canal, and she believes that because she herself would not have hesitated to throw him and Japetus into the water if she could have seen any advantage in it. At the same time she was determined to pull as many people as possible with her over the edge of the quay.

Gradually a general cheeriness spread through the crowd that was following her. The procession itself must have appeared comic, with the bear being led away by its keeper; people along the alley stared first in deep wonder. Only after a while did they feel bold enough to risk shouting. They felt safe because apparently Silas had the wild creature under control. Protected by this, they could act independently.

Gradually, as they neared the canal, others joined them. No one wanted to miss what would be the topic of conversation for a long time to come, and the procession, which had begun quite grimly, gradually became like a carnival. In festive spirit, a woman was going to be drowned. Coarse witticisms were tossed back and forth; in their minds people already saw her splashing and shouting in the almost still, black water. No one dreamed that she stood any chance of escaping that fate, for so many of them shared the same intention and she was all alone.

In the alley by the canal there were open spaces between the barges. As soon as they came to the first space, someone shouted that here, this was fine—here, they could stop right here. Silas stopped, and stopped

240

playing as well, and asked the throng whether they wanted her here.

The answer was a many-voiced "yes."

"Fine," said Silas, sticking his flute down in the neck of his sheepskin coat.

Those closest to him drew back slightly, perplexed. They had certainly not expected to be confronted with the task all at once like that, at least not under these circumstances. The uneasiness spread, people unintentionally stepped on the toes of those standing behind them as they drew back. The bare cobbles between the Horse Crone and her judges swiftly widened to a fairly large expanse, and with a nasty grin she pulled the bear close to her. Now they could just walk right up to her, whoever dared.

Everything became extraordinarily quiet. The cheery cockiness died away; no one would be the first to walk over and grab hold of that huge, bony woman.

But if they could not drown her, they could stone her.

Someone kicked up a cobblestone and flung it toward the Horse Crone, and the idea caught on. Then, in every direction, suddenly men and women could be seen bending down and scratching in the cobbles for weapons.

Sensing the danger, the Horse Crone made a couple of running sorties into the crowd with the bear, and the whole crowd rushed shrieking and squealing further back—but only to kick up more cobbles with even greater eagerness.

The stones fell alarmingly close to her feet.

"Why are you doing that?" Silas asked unexpectedly.

A couple of men and women looked at him in astonishment. What a stupid question!

They were going to kill her.

"You can't do that," Silas told them.

"But we don't want her here."

"And when you have struck her and she falls and lets go of the chain—what then?"

A stone hit the bear, who rose angrily on his hind legs with open jaws.

"Then what will you do?" repeated Silas.

Various hands that were closed around stones were lowered hesitantly.

"But we don't want her here," repeated the man in front of Silas.

"How many children will suffer because of that?"

"Children?"

"All the ones who don't reach safety when the bear breaks loose."

They stopped throwing stones.

"But that's only because you stopped playing," shouted a complaining woman. "She was going to set us on fire."

"No, she wasn't," said Silas. "Not if I'm allowed to decide."

"What? What would you do?"

"Make sure that she sails away on her barge."

The Horse Crone glanced swiftly and sharply at Silas while a questioning silence settled over the crowd.

"Sail away?"

The Horse Crone took the bear by the arm and had

already started to walk off; there was no reason to wait for anything, no reason to give them time to change their minds. Murmuring, the procession followed at some distance.

Down on the barge the Horse Crone stood still in the middle of the deck with the bear, while eager hands loosened the hawsers and cast the loose ends on board. Then, using poles they borrowed from other barges, they shoved the vessel free from the dock, shoved it out until it floated in the canal and was slowly swept out toward the river by the gentle current. The distance to dry land grew greater and greater; the Horse Crone did not budge, just stood there, a dark immobile figure on the barge, solitary, lonely, and disliked. A peculiar feeling of oppression seized Melissa at the sight. After all, the Horse Crone was a human being, but no one seemed to pity the woman out there for the uncertain fate she was drifting to meet. They had got rid of someone undesirable; they had unburdened their lives of a stranger —and had fun in the process. They did not feel responsible for the Horse Crone's future.

"But she's drifting out to sea," whispered Melissa in terror. "She can't get ashore anywhere by herself and the current will carry her far out into the ocean."

"She'll come to lots of towns before she gets to the ocean," Silas consoled her.

Melissa's eyes, otherwise so calm and steady, expressed concern and doubt.

"She'll drift past them," she objected. "The river is wide and she can't land by herself."

"I have never known anything to get the better of

her," said Silas. "She always turns everything to her own advantage."

"Have you known her a long time?" asked Melissa.

Silas calculated and nodded, yes, he felt that he had known her a long time.

Japetus came over and stood by them silently; he too was not at ease. The attempt to stone the woman had made a harrowing impression on him. He still followed the slowly drifting vessel with his eyes, feeling how grateful he was not to belong to that part of town. He felt that he must seem just as strange and disliked to the people there as the woman who was drifting away.

The barge quietly came out of the black canal and was seized by the current and swung around.

"She's strong as an ox," said Silas. "And she has a voice that can make the dead themselves do her errands for her—and anyway, she has her own barge poles on board."

"Still it must be strange," sighed Melissa when the black form had drifted out of sight.

Silas looked at her inquiringly.

"I mean to be like that," said Melissa. "To live that kind of life."

"She would never tolerate living in the same place for any length of time." said Silas. "Nor can I."

"Are you leaving?"

Both Melissa and Japetus turned toward him with a start.

Silas hesitated momentarily.

"I never got to say good-bye to Ben-Godik or anyone else in the village. They don't know where I went. I really had no intention of going off."

The others could understand how he felt and they did not know what to reply.

"Do you have to go right away?" asked Japetus a little later. "After all, you haven't been gone so very long."

"You could also come back," exclaimed Melissa. "You would be welcome to live with us, I'm sure." She grabbed his arm eagerly.

"I'll think it over," promised Silas.

"But you already have a room in our house," said Japetus, somewhat offended. "Mother has said that you can just live there."

Silas looked from one to the other. In a way he had nothing against staying in the town awhile longer; there was a lot he would like to know more about, but on the other hand, he had to ride back to Ben-Godik and tell him that he was neither dead nor in any other kind of trouble—and now, after all, he did have his mare back.

"If I come back I'll definitely not live with either of you," he laughed suddenly.

"Then where?" they both asked simultaneously.

"Try and guess."

Both Melissa and Japetus thought for a long time but neither of them could imagine anywhere else.

"On a river barge," laughed Silas.

For a brief moment their eyes glanced down the canal to the river where the barge had disappeared from sight.

The Author

CECIL BØDKER was born in Denmark in 1927. She grew up in the country, with five brothers. After high school she became a silversmith apprentice and then worked as a silversmith in Denmark and Sweden. In 1955 she published her first book of poetry, followed by novels, short stories, and radio and television plays. SILAS AND THE BLACK MARE, her first children's book, won the Danish Academy Prize for children's literature in 1967. Several more books about Silas and other children's stories brought her many awards, culminating in the 1976 Hans Christian Andersen medal. Cecil Bødker lives on a farm in Jutland with her four daughters, two of whom were adopted in Ethiopia.